REVEALED

A Novel

Mary Unruh Ballard, MD

MARICARM • PRESS

MariCarm • PRESS

This novel is a work of fiction as are the names, characters, places and occurences.
No resemblance is made to any actual persons, alive or dead, events or locations.

Copyright © 2012 by Mary Unruh Ballard, MD

Published by MariCarm Press
718 Griffin Avenue #197
Enumclaw, WA 98022

Printed by Gorham Printing
3718 Mahoney Drive
Centralia, WA 98531 USA

First Edition

ISBN 978-0-9855127-0-5

Edited by Barbara Fandrich
Book Design by Patricia Coppedge
Cover Design by Kathryn E. Campbell
Back Cover Photography by Stephanie Campbell

To *Antonio Vinciguerra,* a sixteenth century Italian poet

   —My ancestor, who passed along to me his writing skills

To *Patrick Allen Dalessandro*

   —My cousin, who has believed in me since the day I was born

To *Alison Mary* and *Michael David*

   —My children, who fill every day of my life with joy

THE EMERGENCY ROOM

"Code red, code red. Security to the emergency room, stat! Code red, code red." The hospital overhead paging system blared the words as Dr. Ralph Peyton flew out of his office just down the hall from the ER triage area. Code red meant a security threat: an out-of-control patient, family member, employee, anyone or anything that threw the hospital into panic mode. He remembered that Dr. Nolan was still on duty from last night and hadn't changed her shift yet. That made him panic even more.

He arrived in time to see glass canisters filled with cotton swabs and plastic emesis trays thrown across the room, crashing against the recently replaced drywall. A half-filled plastic bottle of saline had spilled on the newly waxed floor in the hallway.

"I want my pills, I want my pills!" the patient screamed. His matted black hair did little to cover his bloodshot eyes, which gave away he was twenty-four, maybe forty-eight hours into his withdrawals. The room spun around him and the fluorescent lights overhead made him nauseated. He pulled out his gun from under his grease-stained, hooded jacket, and just as suddenly the woman in front of him grabbed his arm and pulled him closer to her.

Dr. Samantha Nolan cocked back the trigger of the patient's handgun and pushed it up under her chin. The patient tried to stare her down, only to find the dark brown irises of her eyes were now fixed and steady on his every move. His hands grew colder and his white fingers barely maintained their grip on the gun.

"Go ahead! You really think I like this job after treating someone like you?"

The patient, unable to keep beads of sweat from draining down his temples, took a deep swallow. This wasn't what he expected. She wasn't what he expected.

The ER, usually filled with screaming trauma patients, fell silent. Sam breathed in the scent of the last sterile alcohol prep left on the countertop and tried to focus on one spot on the white walls of the hospital she'd called home for the past twenty-three years. The security guard drew his gun and crouched further behind a metal utility cart. He shielded himself from the frozen stances of the nurses and orderlies and the blank stares of the other patients.

The gun-wielding psycho couldn't believe what was happening. When he tried to pull the gun off Sam, she squeezed his hand tighter and dug the metal even deeper into her throat. Sam raised herself up from the floor and took the psycho with her.

"That's it! I spend shift after shift in this hell-hole of an ER, taking nothing but crap from lazy drug addicts like you. I put up with vomit on my clothes, spit on my face, and urine in my hair because you think since I have a medical license, it gives you the right to beat up on me. Then, when I'm done putting lowlifes like you back together, you find some ambulance-chasing lawyer who works out of his briefcase to sue me and raise my malpractice rates through the ceiling because you walked out of the ER against medical advice while you were still high, got in your black pickup truck with the monster wheels and struck a six-year-old kid on your way back to the crack house."

Sam's boss, Dr. Ralph Peyton, watched his favorite colleague from the emergency room doorway. He shook his head. He'd heard it all from her before, in one way or another. Ralph removed the nametag reading "Dr. Ralph Peyton, Chief Medical Officer" from his lapel and placed it in his coat pocket without the perpetrator noticing. Ralph had learned from his early days on the streets of Philadelphia not to draw attention. Ralph was the only person left in hospital administration with enough patience and fortitude to be Sam's supervisor. He'd known months ago this day was going to arrive.

Sam drew the psycho closer to her chest. "Go ahead, shoot me and put me out of my misery, so I don't have to wake up tomorrow and deal with trash like you," Sam shouted into the psycho's face. "Shoot me, you piece of garbage."

The psycho pulled his gun away and threw it against the ER wall.

"Get her off me, get her away from me—she's crazy!"

The SWAT team descended upon the shaken emergency room. The security guard tried to handcuff the psycho, but the psycho clutched the guard with tears of relief. The cleaning crew arrived and started to wipe away the last vestiges of the recent drama, waiting for the next one that probably lay

7

not too far behind. The previously quiet patients, now with a letdown of adrenaline, rediscovered their pains, and cries of muscle aches filled the air again. A heavy-set young man from utilities, a petite blonde, and a wiry black woman put the ER back into its usual ordered chaos.

Ralph gave a sigh of relief and approached his favorite apprentice. "Sam, are you all right?"

"Ralph, I haven't been right since I joined this profession."

Ralph nodded his head in agreement. "Go home, Sam. I'll get Foxworth to finish your shift. Get some rest. I want you in my office tomorrow at eight a.m., sharp."

"Yes sir," Sam replied, at attention.

Ralph gave her one last look. "Sam, that's eight a.m. sharp, and sober."

THE MOUNTAINTOP

Adam Lakeland stopped to watch the early morning sun reach over the mountaintop. The sounds of birds waking up highlighted the silence of the crisp morning air. He could see his breath. There was no wind. The light through the trees showed the hillside as a mosaic of textures. He could only feel warmth against his weather-beaten face. He closed his eyes and breathed. He and his wife, Miranda, were welcoming their first child to Woodbridge, Alaska, where both had grown up. Adam never thought life could be this good, but it was.

Loud chainsaws trimmed the branches from fallen trees that were lying on the ground. Every piece of the forest was loved and respected, and became a part of the livelihood of all the residents in the town. A large evergreen fell slowly to one side, as several of Adam's coworkers cleared the area.

Matt yelled the traditional call, "Clear, timber down!"

The loggers hear that a hundred times a day and never think much about it. Today would be different.

Matt and Connor stayed back from the falling tower, but Adam's boot got caught between two logs as the tree gained momentum.

"Help, anybody, I'm caught!" Adam struggled to pull his leg out of the crevice. He knew he should have bought new boots sooner, but a crib was more important. Matt turned to see Adam about to be crushed right in front of him.

"No, Adam!" The tree made a loud thud as it hit the ground and trapped Adam's lower body. Now Adam felt nothing, no air, no wind, no sunlight, just stillness. Connor and Matt rushed to Adam.

"Is he alive?" Connor made the sign of the cross as Matt checked Adam's pulse.

"Barely. I'll stay with him. Get the others and get into town for some help."

Connor took off down the side of the mountain, scattering rock and brush along the way, and Adam's flailing arm reached out to Matt as he whispered, "God, help me, please. I want to see my baby."

"I'm with you, buddy. I'm here," Matt answered. He took the chainsaw and started cutting Adam out.

THE SAW MILL

It was the sound that everyone in town feared the most. The warning whistle started to blow and everyone stopped in their tracks, counting off the number of whistles. Five, six, then seven long whistles. They knew something bad had happened. The loggers at base camp dropped what they were doing and started running up the hillside, yelling for everyone who was available to come out and help.

Miranda Lakeland felt her pregnant belly touch the floor, which now smelled of pine from her intense scrubbing. She rose, one foot on the floor and then the other to steady herself. Time seemed to grind into slow motion with the sound of the seventh whistle. She took three long steps to the window and stared at the mountaintop. She squeezed the cross on her necklace in her hand, while she calmed her growing belly with the other.

The loggers made it to the mountaintop and released Adam. Jack Byron, an older, brawny logger, had already made it to Adam. He knew this site before. His own limp reflected the leg he had sacrificed to this same mountaintop. She was a beauty of a mountain: loved, revered, and respected, but feared at the same time.

"Get that stretcher up here now, while he's still alive." Jack could see Adam trying to talk.

"I can't breathe, Jack, it hurts too much."

"Take my hand, Adam, and squeeze it all you can. Just keep breathing."

Adam fought to keep his eyes open. "If I don't make it, Jack, tell Miranda I love her and our baby." Jack knelt down closer. Adam's once brawny chest was now barely moving.

"Knock it off, Adam, you'll be home before dinner. You can tell her yourself then." Jack bit the edge of his lip so hard it started bleeding.

"Let's go, guys. Get these logs off him."

The loggers pulled Adam out and onto a stretcher. Connor stood at Adam's head and panicked. "He doesn't have a pulse! My God, he's blue, Jack!"

Adam felt colder and the voices around him started to sound softer.

The loggers began CPR as they rushed Adam down the mountain. The morning fog, which had cleared earlier, started to move in again.

THE EARTH ABIDETH FOREVER

Jamie Logan's sweet voice singing "Amazing Grace" could be heard throughout the entire Woodbridge Valley. Miranda cradled a mound of dirt from the mountaintop and threw it onto Adam's grave. She gently stroked her belly.

"Rest well, my love. I will make sure our child knows you." The townspeople filed past to wish her well, mostly the women. The men stood in the background, afraid to step too close to Adam's grave. Death on the mountaintop was always on the back of their minds. They wanted it to stay that way.

Skye Ronan stood alone overlooking the valley, head down and arms folded across his broad chest. He picked up a rock and raised back his muscular arm, throwing it down into the crevice of trees and shrub. The anger in Skye's release made it skip into the brush until it could no longer be seen or heard.

Skye and Jack approached Ray Connelly, the silver-haired patriarch and owner of White River Logging Company. Ray knew these men like the back of his hand. It was hard enough to lose a coworker, but for them to lose someone they'd grown up with, laughed and drank and fought with, and married off to Ray's long-time sweetheart, it would take longer than an eternity of time to heal their wounds.

"Ray, we can't go on like this anymore. If we had a doctor at basecamp, Adam would be alive," Skye insisted.

"I know, Skye. I don't need the hooktender of my own company to tell me that. I've been pleading with the mayor for years."

Jack furrowed his graying brow. This usually warned the guys that an unanswered question was soon to follow. Not only did Ray know his men, but through many years of gentle, and not always gentle bantering, they knew him.

"Besides, where are we going to get a doctor crazy enough to come out here?"

THE APARTMENT

Sam lifted each foot, like a ten-ton weight, up the steps to her apartment building door. It seemed like an hour just to get to the top of the concrete steps. She rustled through her leather bag for her keys and came across the armband of the psycho patient from the ER the night before. She grabbed it and threw it in the outside trash, entered the foyer, and quickly shut the door behind her, trying to shut out the past twenty-four hours. She carefully placed her feet on the black diamond pattern of the tile floor, so as not wake any of her neighbors. Six a.m. was fine for her, it meant she was off work and sleep was soon to follow.

Her brass key slid effortlessly into her mailbox door, and she quietly opened the metal cover and pulled out an envelope addressed to "Dr. Sam." There was no stamp or return address, and she wondered how someone had gotten into the building to drop this in her box. Hank, the super, lectured the residents incessantly about not letting anyone unknown into the building.

Suddenly, Tommy Sanford, sporting a new Mohawk designer haircut, burst into the foyer with his titanium bicycle. Any hope of rest and relaxation for the renters was now gone; morning had officially broken.

"Hey, hey, Dr. Sam. Big night at the crazy house?"

Sam sighed as she riffled through her mail. "Tommy boy, just another day serving the public good."

Sam first opened the envelope without a stamp or return

address label. The outside of the card read "Happy Father's Day." Puzzled, she couldn't match Father's Day to the current season. She lifted the front of the card and the inside verse read simply "MURDERER," written by hand.

Tommy secured his helmet, then noticed Sam's quiet stance. "Love letter from a fan?"

She hadn't even looked up at Tommy when the rest of her mail went tumbling through her hands onto the floor. The advertising postcards flew across the enclosed space and, stopped only by the inside door leading to the apartment homes.

Sam knelt down. "Uh, something like that."

"You okay, Sam?" Tommy waited for Sam to look up.

"Sure. Tommy, Father's Day is still in June, right?"

"Yeah, that was three months ago." Tommy paused.

"Right." Sam forced a smile. "Everybody knows that."

Tommy picked up the last of Sam's mail and handed it to her. "You need help in, Doc?" He stood, waiting for an answer.

"No, of course not, go on, Tommy."

The young man left the front of the building with his bicycle. Sam leaned her exhausted shoulders against the cold marble wall. She stood there quietly, the warm morning sun streaming through the cut glass of the ceiling windows reflecting the sheen of the black and white floor tiles. In spite of the warmth she shivered under her coat.

THE RESTAURANT

Natalee, "Nin" Butler had been Sam's best friend for over twenty years. Nin had seen Sam grow from a lamb of a junior hospital associate to one of the most well-respected doctors in the Pacific Northwest. She'd also seen Sam become one of the most outspoken critics of hospital policy, much to the delight of her patients and residents of the community, and much to the fear of hospital administration.

On this sunny morning Nin clutched the morning paper under her arm, hardly even noticing the parade of fire trucks and sirens streaming past her. While she waited for her habitually late friend to show up, she sipped her orange juice at the café table. She'd ordered her regular large glass, more pulp that way.

Joanie's Café was just down the block from the hospital. Sam and Nin were regular fixtures, and seemingly always at the same table. The waiters and waitresses could set their clocks by Sam's arrival, as it meant the end of another shift at the hospital. Nin checked her watch. She was halfway through her orange juice, when she saw Sam rushing into the front of the café. Nin knew better than to order a Mimosa for breakfast; she was trying to help Sam as much as she could. Help was never something that Sam took to kindly, and Nin knew that help had to be given as an invisible net, a caring force in the background of a dear friendship, stable and always present.

Sam arrived. A gentle smile lit up Nin's face.

"Get over here, doctor lady." Nin hugged Sam as the waiter arrived.

"Tomato juice, please, and I'm not ready to order yet," Sam declared to the waiter. Her doctor persona hadn't shaken off yet from the night's emergency room shift.

"No vodka with that tomato juice, per chance?" Nin inquired.

"I'm happily four months now. Are you requesting a drug test?" Sam set her purse on the chair next to them.

"You were the one who told me to be ruthless. I'm just keeping my promise," Nin reminded her.

The waiter brought Sam's tomato juice in a tall glass with a celery stick. Sam fondly recalled her Bloody Mary days, and also remembered too many times Nin had sobered her up with fluids and crackers before dropping her off at the front door of the ER in her scrubs, ready to start the next shift.

"Your tomato juice, ma'am." The waiter couldn't help but wink.

"Thanks," Sam replied. The young waiter, blonde, with several piercings in his left ear, hesitated and took up a permanent stop by Sam's side.

Sam looked up from her tomato juice. "Thank you, young man. I'm still not ready to order, and I'm old enough to be your mother." The waiter's disappointed smile followed him to the kitchen station where he filled drinks for the next customers.

"You're no fun, Sam. He looks like he could be a really bad boy."

Sam pulled the Father's Day card out of her handbag and handed it to Nin.

"What do you make of this, Nin? I found it in my mailbox this morning."

Nin opened the card. She started reading it, then paused and got her glasses out of her handbag. She couldn't believe the inside message. She waited to respond to Sam, not wanting to appear unnerved, knowing that would be contagious. Sam already had plenty to worry about, getting back on track with her job after her rehab stint. Nin did what she does best, and kept things light.

"I think you've been workin' in that ER rat hole way too much." Nin noticed the young waiter continuing to set his sights on Sam. "And you need to get out and get laid more often."

Sam sat stone-faced, not responding to Nin's usual banter.

"You have got to have the filthiest mouth for a social worker I have ever heard. But tell me what you think of this. I mean it, this card gives me the creeps."

"Any late night hang-ups, footsteps in the hospital parking lot?" Nin asked with a shudder.

"No." Sam didn't see what difference that should make. It still nagged at her peace of mind.

"Then let it go—hospitals get crazies all the time."

Nin spotted Sam's keys on the table and picked them up. The tattered photo of Sam with her ex-boyfriend, Pete, never really fit quite right in the plastic holder. Nothing ever fit with Pete.

"You can always call Detective Pete O'Halloran, the brave ex-boyfriend, slash, Irish cop. He doesn't carry a torch for you, it's more like a burning building on his shoulders."

Sam had completely forgotten she still had Pete's photo on her keychain, and she grabbed it from Nin.

"It crossed my mind, but I won't do that to him." Her eyes lowered.

"But you will keep his photo on your keychain?" Nin's mocking smile took up residence on her face. When it came to guys, Sam needed a push, no, a healthy shove.

"I'm just not ready to put it away," Sam confessed. A confession that didn't feel good for the soul. She felt that sinking feeling in the pit of her stomach that sits between a yes and a no, hoping some great force in the universe would make that decision for her.

"What are you ready for, Sam? I'd really like to know." Nin stood her ground.

The waiter returned and stood between the two fair maidens. He leaned to one side and put his hand on his hip, waiting for an answer, any answer from Sam.

"I'm ready...to order."

DR. RALPH PEYTON'S OFFICE

Ralph Peyton sat behind his mahogany desk with his personal medical library of thirty years squeezed into the bookshelves behind him. The far wall was nearly completely filled with diplomas, licensing credentials, and achievement awards; Villanova Undergrad, Jefferson Medical College, University of Pennsylvania, and Ralph's personal favorite, the 1969 Black

Student Scholar Athlete Award from the Philadelphia Chamber of Commerce. Ralph wondered if his boxing skills would be needed this morning to go at another round with Sam. He heard that notorious loud, aggressive knock at the door.

"Come on in, Sam. I know your knock." Ralph's voice could be heard down the hall.

Sam entered the room with her hair pulled back and face scrubbed, ready to defend herself. "How do you always know that it's me? May I sit down, or do you want me to take a breathalyzer first?"

Ralph put his glasses back on. He knew they would make him look more authoritarian. He figured he might as well give it a try, despite the fact that Sam didn't respect authority anyway. It was worth the minimal effort.

"You are four months sober now, my dear. Congratulations. I personally always knew you could do it."

Sam sat in the chair across from Ralph, out of Ralph's direct gaze. Though she was tempted, she restrained herself from resting her foot on the front of his desk. The desk from which he commanded the department with a combination of discipline and fatherly empathy.

"You are the all-seeing and all-knowing one, Ralph."

"And what I see, Sam, is a little off-balance right now." Ralph leaned back in his chair to stretch.

Sam straightened the pictures on Ralph's desk. Her OCD traits always came to the surface when she got nervous. Ralph gazed at Sam and raised his right eyebrow. Ralph waited until Sam stopped what she was doing and put her hands back in her lap. He wasn't going to let her get away with her usual stalling techniques. He wanted her full and complete attention. With Sam, it was like trying to chase a moth off the ceiling into a miniature glass jar.

"So I got a little flamboyant in the ER—I handled the situation." Sam's hands flapped in the air.

"Sam, a gun-wielding psycho in our illustrious emergency room screamed and yelled for security to protect him from one of our emergency room physicians. Do you see anything wrong with this picture, if I may ask?"

Sam attempted to lean forward and place her elbow on the desk as a chin rest. Ralph lowered his eyeglasses. Sam withdrew, and squeezed the armrests of her chair. She was moving more, so she knew she was not going to like what she was about to hear.

"You've had three disciplinary write-ups in the past six months, CEO Clyde calls me every other day wondering when I am going to can you, and if it weren't for the fact that you take care of half of the Board of Directors of this hospital, and their children and their wives, you would have been gone over a year ago."

Sam managed to crack a smile, not too wide.

"My, my, my, you are so busy keeping track of one girl, Ralph."

Ralph took off his glasses and shoved them into his shirt pocket, rather than tear them apart. His breathing became heavier. Sam could see that vein dilate on his forehead, the one that signaled there could only be a little more he could take before his head exploded.

"Sam, my blood pressure is taking a trip to Canada."

"Okay, Ralph, I'll practice my deep breathing exercises and

try a little harder next time. In fact, I'll sign up for a yoga class, start to meditate and become a vegetarian. Will that keep you and Frog-Eyes Clyde happy? I swear he's related to Kermit."

Ralph yanked open his top file drawer, almost tipping over the entire cabinet. He threw a stack of papers in front of Sam in a file marked "Alaska." Sam sat up in her chair and turned the file toward her. She didn't pick it up but looked at the label.

"Alaska? Are you my supervisor or my travel agent."

"Read up on it. Woodbridge Logging Company's been bugging the hospital for three months to send them one of our physicians to start a clinic. As per my conversation with the higher-ups this morning, you just got drafted."

"Alaska! This is a joke, right?"

Ralph leaned back in his chair, tipping it against the wall behind him. He clasped his hands behind his neck and returned his own smile back to Sam.

"You aren't serious about sending me up there, Ralph! It's nothing but a bunch of redneck loggers, crazy fishermen, and Vitamin D deficient locals who don't see the sun twenty-three hours a day. Oh no, not even you would stoop this low."

Ralph's smile accelerated to a complete facial grin.

"Clyde says it's the wide open spaces for you, or the wide open door out of your job."

"I'm not goin'." Sam started putting all the loose paper clips on Ralph's desk back into the paper clip bin.

Ralph got up and walked over to the door of his office.

"I know that one-third of alcoholics have obsessive-compulsive disorder and you can rearrange my desk all you want, but it won't help."

21

Ralph shut the door before Sam had a chance to leave. Ralph's tall frame leaned against the inside of the door, and his voice softened.

"Sam, I mean it this time. Clyde wants your head. I promised him after your rehab there wouldn't be anything else. With the ER incident, now there is something else. You're the best I've got in this place; please consider this."

Sam listened to her own advice and took a long, deep breath.

"No, for now."

Ralph opened the door to the hallway.

"Come on, there's someone I want you to meet."

RAY CONNELLY

Ray Connelly sat on a parson's bench in the hallway outside Ralph's office. He wasn't used to wearing a suit in his line of work. He got up and started pacing the hallway to loosen his clothes. It didn't help. Why did Millie put so much starch in his collar? He wasn't in Catholic school anymore and there sure weren't any nuns around. He had to work at keeping his normally baritone voice low so his cell phone conversation wouldn't disturb any of the other offices. He saw Ralph and a woman walking toward him. Ralph's pace was much faster than hers. She looked like she was already waiting for a chance to escape.

"Yeah, I gotta go, Skye. I'll call back in ten minutes." He turned his phone off and stuck it in his polyester coat pocket.

"You the logging camp owner?" Sam asked, extending a handshake to Ray. She squeezed his hand so hard he winced.

Ray held Sam's hand for an extra second, then let go. He liked a good, strong grip. Sam looked him straight in the eye. She wasn't going to show him any fear, though her backbone felt differently.

"Twenty-one years now, ma'am."

Ralph stuck his hands in his pants pockets, which were hidden by his jacket. He stood an equal distance between Ray and Sam. It was time for him to be polite and keep his mouth shut.

"I told Sam you need a doctor at the logging camp, especially one with her experience."

"Great. What experience have you had?" Ray watched Sam fold her arms across her chest. He'd been working with strapping loggers for years and knew the meaning of that stance.

"Last night I grabbed the arm of some psycho patient and shoved his pistol up my chin." Sam moved her arms from across her chest and put her hands on her hips while waiting for an answer from Ray.

Ralph, as always with Sam, shook his head.

"Sounds like you'll fit right into Alaska, ma'am." Ray kept himself from smiling too big.

"No, I don't think so. Interesting meeting you, Mr. Connelly, but I have to prepare for a lecture I'm giving tonight." Sam threw on her coat and darted toward the stairs.

"She really does grow on you," Ralph reassured Ray, who by now was halfway to the stairs himself.

"'Risk factors for cardiac disease in blue collar workers,' right?" Ray said, reciting the name of Sam's lecture.

Sam turned and tightened the belt on her coat.

This time Ray extended his hand to Sam. "Not bad for a redneck, eh?"

Ray sat in the back of the audience in the hospital auditorium and watched Sam point to the screen. It was the one part of the hospital that didn't smell like freshly waxed floors, but it was still sterile: white walls, white coats on the doctors, and white clogs on the nurses. He was anxious to get back to Woodridge and see color again. The deep green trees and blue skies felt a million miles away. He kept trying to figure out a way he could just get this doctor there.

"And in conclusion, it is imperative for the healthcare provider to screen blue collar workers for deeper sources of stress and anxiety as part of the cardiac exam. Thank you, everyone, for your attention." Sam heard half the audience clap and saw the other half wake up from the clapping.

Ray was the first one to the front of the room. Sam didn't look up. She grabbed her computer carrier and started stuffing her computer and cords into the bag. She pressed the button on the podium that raised the screen upward. It felt like it was taking forever for the screen to retract.

Come on, she thought. The longer I stand here the better chance he has to corner me.

Time drifted into slow motion. She saw Ray moving in and nowhere for her to go.

"Dr. Nolan, we could really use some of your doctoring at

the camp. You never know, you might actually like it up there," Ray persisted. He picked up the computer bag.

"I have gunshot wounds, stabbings, every broken bone one could see, right here in my backyard; why would I want to give up all this?" Sam turned out the lights of the auditorium and led Ray out.

"Because you never know where you'll find your real adventure."

"Are you working me, Mr. Connelly?" Sam threw her handbag over her shoulder. She took a barrette out of her hair and let it all drift down to her shoulders. Her day was done and she was outta here, with or without this guy.

"It's Ray, and let me walk you to your car."

Sam saw the mosquitos circle the lights of the hospital parking lot. She could hear the crickets in the shrubs in the distance, serenading in unison. This meant to her that the last vestiges of summer were coming to an end, and fall would soon be here. There were only two cars left, in close proximity, her BMW and what she assumed was Ray's rig. She slowed down the pace of her walk so Ray could keep up with her. Ray stopped at a rented Buick. A GM man to the core. It fit.

Ray struggled with the car door opener, but finally got it to beep the right way and opened his driver's side door.

"I'm leaving to go back to Woodbridge tomorrow. Is there anything I can say or do to change your mind about not going?" Ray rarely pleaded, but he knew he couldn't go home empty-handed. Not only the loggers, but the whole town had their hopes riding on him to bring her back.

25

Sam thought she heard a noise in the shadow of the nearby bushes, but she couldn't make out if there were footsteps.

"Not at this point," Sam replied, distracted. "My life is here, not a great life but it's all I've got."

"Maybe for now, Dr. Nolan, but that's only today. Here's my card, keep it somewhere where you won't lose it or throw it away." Ray got in the Buick and started it up. Not the powerful engine of his pickup, but he guessed it was enough for businessmen in fine suits.

Sam held the card in her hand while Ray lowered his window.

"I can't make any promises," she said.

Ray fumbled to turn on the headlights. "You will."

Ray drove off. The taillights of his car blended in with the last lights of the parking lot while Sam stood alone. She looked behind her right shoulder and thought she heard a snap. When she turned, she could see a fresh bud had fallen onto the ground. She took Ray's business card and got ready to tear it up, but put it in her coat pocket instead. As she drove off, a smoldering cigarette butt fell on the ground next to the rosebud.

THE HOSPITAL LIBRARY

Sam sat at the metal table and brushed the coffeecake crumbs into the rusted trashcan. It must have been a late evening into the morning for last night's ER doc. The more crumbs, the more admissions, the more eating to stay awake. At least it hadn't been her. Her table started to wobble as she moved around in her seat. You would think with all the money this hospital wasted on administrators, they could buy the doctors decent tables for their library, but then again, Clyde was the CEO. She stared at Ray's business card in front of her. She picked it up and started flicking it with her fingers when she heard a book drop to the floor in the shelves behind her. She stretched her neck to take a look.

"Is anyone there?"

Sam tried to focus back on her "interesting" reading, Treatment of Patients with Congenitally Absent Uvulas. It was just enough to wake her up.

Her colleague, Dr. Daniel Markus, stepped out from behind the bookshelves. Markus wore enough gel in his hair that Sam always feared she would slide across the room if she got too close to him. She never had any smidgeon of desire to get too close to Markus, much to his chagrin.

"Just can't stay out of controversy, can you, Sam?" Markus checked his mailbox and shoved his New England Journal of Medicine under his arm. He couldn't resist checking his hairstyle in the stainless steel coffeepot as he passed by Sam.

"I'm almost as good at it as you are, Markus. It's just harder for me to sleep with every nurse on the medical floor."

Markus laughed and leaned over Sam. "Maybe, but at least I'm trying." Markus hustled out the door before she could throw her stethoscope at him.

Sam slammed shut the textbook she was reading. She sat alone, mulling over whether to get another cup of coffee before she had to go back on shift. It was late in the day. She figured it was the same pot from 6 a.m. this morning that the guy on call last night had made. There wasn't enough coffee creamer and sugar in the universe to make it taste decent.

Sam put her head down on the table and closed her eyes. Just a few more minutes of relaxation before she had to go back to "the pit," as she affectionately called the ER. The chair at the table next to her fell over. Sam went to pick it up, and before she was halfway standing a sea of books came rushing toward her like a concrete wave. She rolled herself over and barely got her leg away from the wreckage. She sat there for a minute and watched the last of the books settling into the splinters of what previously were the wooden shelves. That minute felt like an hour.

PETE O'HALLORAN

Sam hadn't been to the police station in months, maybe even as long as a year. Had it really been that long since she and Pete had stopped seeing each other? She loved the old station with its turn-of-the-century gaslights and how the hardwood floors creaked with the endless traffic of people: cops, bad guys, and everyone else in between.

Bill O'Brien, affectionately known to her as "O.B." had over thirty years at the reception desk. The department couldn't imagine anyone but O.B. running this place. He ran it with an iron hand. That's what it took. Sam loved everything about O.B., his thick, gray hair, endless smile, and even his paunch of a belly. He looked like he had the map of Ireland written all over his face.

"Dr. Sam! We needed some sunlight in this place; it's been too long."

"O.B., I should come visit more often just so you can feed my ego." Sam smiled then looked over O'Brien's desk and her smile gently faded when she saw Pete O'Halloran talking to another officer.

Sam first met Pete when he was investigating a gunshot victim Sam had treated in the emergency room. Even today, he still had those steel blue eyes that reflect the light by day and settle into a deep ocean blue at night. Sam coughed to stop her heart from skipping a few beats. O.B. peered at Sam over his wire-rimmed glasses.

"We really miss your visits." O.B. gestured over his shoulder to Pete. "We really do. We talk about you all the time. In fact, I think we even eat, sleep, and dream Dr. Sam."

"I wish this were a social visit, O.B., but I actually think someone is following me."

"Anyone you think you know?" O.B. turned serious. Sam was the daughter he'd never had. He'd always been protective of her and this time he sensed her fear.

Sam watched Pete in mid-conversation. Before she could look away, Pete saw her standing there. The pupils of his eyes widened into his blue iris.

"Don't know. Any suggestions on what I should do?" Sam pulled herself away from Pete's gaze and tried to focus back on O.B.

"Here, let's start with a report. I'll make sure it gets to Taylor. The guy's a flea, he sticks to everything."

"Thanks, O.B."

Pete lifted a finger to interrupt his coworker. "Can you give me a minute."

Pete walked over to Sam. She had forgotten how his 6'4" frame towered over her.

"Hi, Sam. It's been long, too long. How are you?"

"I'm okay, sort of." Sam clutched her shoulder bag closer to her chest.

Pete brushed his straight, dark bangs to one side.

"I was hoping you were coming to see me."

"Work, you know how it gets in the way." Sam tried to button the top of her coat, but she couldn't get the button in the hole.

"I guess for some people." Pete pursed his lips. He undid the top button of his white shirt, next to his collar, and loosened his tie.

"Can I take you for coffee? I know better than to say drinks."

Sam was always a sucker for Pete's sincerity. She'd hurt him so much, she just didn't have the heart to say no. She figured she still needed a little closure herself.

"Let me go home and clean up, I'll meet you at—"
"Randall's Grill," Pete chimed in before she could finish her sentence. "I remember all your favorite places."

❧

It was early evening, and Sam couldn't quite decide if the fluorescent lights over the mirror or the last trickle of daylight was better for getting ready. She remembered it was Pete she was going to see and settled on the daylight and the shadows that went with it. She struggled to get her earring to cooperate, which always seemed to happen when she was going to meet Pete. There was always some kind of obstacle somewhere when it came to Pete.

The phone rang. Sam gave up on the earring and answered it. "Hello? Hello, Pete, is that you?"

The click of the hang-up on the other end of the phone became a monotonous dial tone. Sam skipped the earrings and left for the restaurant.

Like always, she was running late. She finally made it to the entrance of the restaurant and scanned the hungry faces. The sweet smell of charbroiled burgers could not settle the butterflies in her stomach. Guess it was going to be a bottomless glass of iced tea and chicken soup again. The impending presence of Pete made her slip back into her old patterns.

The stick-thin waiter noticed Sam bobbing her head and looking around the room.

"Can I seat you, miss?"

Sam focused immediately on the young waiter. "I'm supposed to meet someone. Did you just call me miss, not ma'am?"

"Why, yes—I'm sorry if I offended you." He hesitated.

"Thank you, young man. I haven't been called 'miss' in over ten years."

Sam saw Pete at a back table. Why does Pete always stick us away from everyone? She remembered his style. The walk to Pete seemed a million miles away and hours long. Pete's cell phone rang. He stared at Sam, then clicked off his phone before she got to the table. There would be no interruptions between them. He was determined to make sure of that.

"Sorry, you know me." Sam slid into the chair across from Pete, careful not to sit next to him. Pete had her tea waiting.

"I always thought the opposite. I always thought the problem between us was that I didn't know you." He wasn't going to waste any time.

Sam glanced toward the front of the restaurant.

"Where is the waiter when you need him most?"

"I'm a little concerned about what brought you to the precinct today. Any way I can help?" Pete fixed his gaze on Sam for an answer.

"O.B.'s on it; they'll look into it. You trying to be the knight in shining armor again?"

"Funny you of all people should say that. I always thought you wore the armor in our relationship."

"I never intended to hurt you, Pete." She tried to squirt the lemon wedge into her drink, but the juice flew all over the table. Her lack of graciousness spread from table manners to boyfriends.

"True, but you did. How long has it been, Sam? Three, four months now, and not one word from you. I thought you needed space, not time."

"To be honest, I'm not sure what I need, Pete."

Pete pulled a pack of cigarettes out of his pants pocket. He remembered he couldn't light up. He knew what was coming next.

"I thought you quit those cancer sticks?"

"I did. Then I failed. I figure I'll try to quit again, then again, then again. A very wise doctor once told me that to successfully quit I have to keep trying again and again, then eventually, I'll succeed."

"Anybody I know?" Sam put her hands on the table. She started tapping the cold glass of tea.

"I'm still trying, Sam. I want to try again." Pete waited.

Sam fussed with her hair.

"Maybe your doctor friend gave you bad advice because she didn't know what to say to you."

Pete gulped down the last of his coffee in true cop style. He threw a few dollars on the table, turned his cell phone back on, and started to leave.

"How does the phrase go…'physician heal thyself.'"

Pete's broad shoulders melted into the glare of the sun as he walked out the front door of the restaurant. Sam stayed at the table and sipped her iced tea.

THE PHOTO

Sam came running downstairs into her apartment foyer with her coat half on when she saw the letter taped to her mailbox. It was getting colder outside and every time the front door of the lobby opened, another gust of air ran a shudder down her spine. Not as much as seeing the letter. She lifted up her collar to feel more secure before she opened the envelope. It was a photo of a cemetery with gravestones in the snow. Her better judgment told her to throw it away right there, but she turned it over. "Bound in life and in death." She let out a deep sigh, and couldn't even get all the air out of her lungs against the stiff enclosure of her coat. She tucked the photo into her left pocket, on the opposite side from where she kept her keys and photo of Pete. Why her, why now? She pushed open the front door of her building only to be engulfed by darkness.

Sam squinted her eyes to capture what light she could in the call room. It was quiet, and she didn't want to turn on the lights. She liked it this way, being the only person in there. She took in the aroma of burnt coffee. They'd left her the mess to clean up, like always. She threw away the rancid coffee grounds and dumped the old coffee in the sink in the bathroom, the men's bathroom. She pulled the gourmet coffee out of her locker and took in a deep whiff, relishing its freshness. Now, this was the way coffee ought to smell. Doctors and coffee, like peanut butter and jelly, but she was tired of the back-to-back shifts, crazy patients, and even crazier hospital administrators. Decent coffee was the one nice thing she did for herself in this gutter she called a hospital.

The steam from the brewing coffee filled the air with the memory of the last trip she and Nin had taken to Italy three years ago. Coffee from Tuscany, now that's the life. What a dear and devoted friend Nin had been all these years, never wavering from listening to Sam complain about her job, her men, or her obsessions.

She sat in the wooden chair, fidgeting to change positions, but couldn't get comfortable and gave up. She stared at the photo of the cemetery in front of her. Who was this and what were they trying to say? She called Nin and figured she would catch her just finishing up at the counseling center.

"Nin, it freaks me out, a cemetery photo."

"You filed a police report, Sam. What else do you want to do?"

Sam took the photo off the table and started tapping it on her knee.

"I think I want to buy a gun."

"Great, so the stalker can shoot you with it?" Nin knew better than to hold back with Sam. It would be the same, if not harsher, if the situation were reversed.

"Meet me at Tumwell's Gun Shop when I get off shift. Please, Nin." Nin heard Sam's voice trail off. Sam never asked for help if she could avoid it. It was hard to see her best friend shaken, not a common sight.

Sam picked at the edge of the photo and laid it across her hand. She could hear Nin's relenting sigh over the other end of the phone.

"Okay, but we'll only go to look, no compulsive shopping."

"I'll be waiting out in front…'Bye."

Sam hung up. She used the photo to scratch the side of her temple. The sharp edge gave her a paper cut.

THE GUN SHOP

Sam stood as still and lifeless as a statue outside Tumwell's Gun Shop, scanning the pedestrians for Nin. She coughed from the cloud of smoke that wandered into her path. It seemed like everyone in the crowd had a cigarette in their hand. Thank God there was a cool breeze that day. She felt light, like there was no temperature in the air. Nin's frantic wave could be seen a half block away. It was Nin's signature wave that meant she had something special to tell Sam. Time and years only bonded their friendship more.

"Let's go in. I don't have much time. I'm meeting some trader for dinner and drinks. I have to catch him while he has money, before his IPO goes bust."

Nin's everyday life provided Sam with the sheer entertainment she missed from being overworked by the emergency room. She didn't need to tape soap operas. She just had to call Nin every now and then to grab coffee and gossip.

They wandered into the gun shop. The light of the outside day faded into a gray room. The closed shutters of the front window provided a sleek barrier from the activity of the outside sidewalk. The musty smell of the glass cases made Sam take a deep breath in and out to get used to the hundreds of new and used guns on display. The store's owner, Jack Tumwell, stepped from behind the counter with a futile attempt to hide his beer gut. He rarely got attractive women in his shop.

"Can I help you ladies find something?" Jack tilted his head to the side to show what hair he had left.

"My friend, Annie Oakley here, thinks she wants a gun for protection," Nin chimed in with a smile.

"The name's Sam. I just need something for nighttime. I live alone and work at a hospital."

Sam continued to stand in the center of the store, while Nin leaned over the glass case. Nin put her handbag on the floor and scanned the various guns on the bottom shelf.

"For when she walks to and from her car in the hospital parking lot or when she wants to terrorize drug-addicted patients in the emergency room."

"You'll need a license, for the gun that is," Tumwell said.

Tumwell tried to straighten up the displays as best as he could to make the place look more presentable. Sales had been slow lately. He needed to make a good appearance with what customers he got. Tumwell's belt clamored with metal from all the keys on his keychain. He sifted through them, sounding like a wind chime in a hurricane until he came upon a small, sharp brass key. He opened the back of the display case and took out two guns.

"This one's a Smith and Wesson and is an older model. Easy to use, but noisy."

Nin grabbed Sam's arm and walked her to the counter. "I don't know, Sam, it might wreak havoc on the uptight neighbors."

Sam flashed Nin her well-practiced angry smile, and slowly built up to "Knock it off."

The gun shop owner reached for a smaller gun and placed

it on top of the glass counter right in front of Sam. Sam couldn't step backward because Nin was behind her.

"I like this one for the ladies, a Colt, small, light, and you can carry it in your pocket or purse, never misses." Tumwell picked it up and extended it toward Sam. "Here, try it."

Sam hesitated, but picked up the gun anyway. She held it in both her hands. It felt like the weight of the world to her. The slickness of the steel slipped through her fingers and she almost dropped the gun out of her hands. She moved it around, but no angle or position felt comfortable to her. Nin and Tumwell watched Sam examine the gun like a patient, without emotion or judgment. Nin leaned forward over Sam's shoulder.

"How does it feel to put something exciting in your hands again?"

"I'm not sure." Sam just stared at the gun. She put it down, then pushed it toward Tumwell.

Tumwell started chewing hard on his gum. He needed to close the deal. His rent was due in three days. "I'll give you twenty percent off if you buy it by the end of the week."

"It's on sale, Sam. Real women never pay full price for anything." Nin could tell they needed a little levity in the situation. She was always good for that. Welcome or not.

Sam shook her head back and forth, then headed for the front door, leaving Nin behind to contend with Tumwell.

"She gets like this. It's her line of work. All those late evenings into the morning without any sleep."

Nin couldn't resist with Tumwell standing right there. Tumwell stood with his mouth wide open while the telephone rang off the hook.

Sam opened the front door and rushed onto the sidewalk. She stepped away from the shop to get as close to the curb as she could get, without being struck by a bus. Nin joined her and waved for a taxi as it started to rain.

"My God, Nin, I save lives for a living and I'm thinking about buying a gun."

"You're scared, Sam. I've never seen you like this." Nin wasn't used to being the rock in the relationship. Sam was always the sturdy one. It unnerved Nin to see the roles switch. Not a common occurrence in their friendship.

Sam pulled her hood up over her head as the rain intensified. Listening to the honking cars and sounds of water streaking onto the sidewalks from noisy buses made her focus less on her shaking hands.

"Some days I don't see me anymore." Sam softened her tone.

The taxi pulled up and Nin got in.

"Gotta fly. Call me tomorrow night for a late movie."

Sam went back to Tumwell's and perused the specials in the gun shop window one more time. She decided to skip the bus and walk back to her apartment.

Pete had always loved to watch Sam walk. Even when she wasn't in a hurry, he sensed her determination in her stride. But today her usual brisk movements were replaced by a slower pace. As she turned the corner two blocks down, Pete flicked his cigarette on the sidewalk and went across the street to the gun shop.

The high-pitched bell jingled back and forth against the window in the gun shop doorway.

"Can I help you, sir?" Tumwell could spot a cop a mile away, with or without the badge.

"Just looking around." Pete scanned the walls for the proverbial gun license, and Tumwell scanned as well to make sure it was in plain sight and up to date. Pete eyed the two guns on the countertop that Sam had looked at.

"These are both beauties; you keep good stock here." Pete picked up the Colt and lifted it up and down in the palm of his hand, feeling the weight of the steel. "And real sturdy too."

"Last customer was looking at that one. Young woman, Pam, Sam, something." Tumwell kept his eye on Pete. He thought it odd that a cop would be snooping around a gun shop when he already had a department issue weapon. Maybe he wasn't looking for himself. He started polishing the Smith and Wesson, holding it like a prized girlfriend.

"She seemed a little on edge, wanted it for protection. I think someone is following her."

Pete cradled the Colt in his hands. "Happens a lot these days," he said, without looking up. He aimed it at a far wall. "This would probably do it. I think my girlfriend would like it. I work a lot of swing shifts."

Tumwell spit his gum into the nearby wastebasket.

"Sold. Here's our list of gun training classes you can give her and an application for a gun permit." Tumwell reached for his filing cabinet before he was interrupted by Pete.

"I'll make sure she gets everything she needs." Pete pulled out his wallet and paid in cash.

THE HOSPITAL

Wendella Lewis had been a fixture at the ER reception desk for over twenty years. She had seen many doctors come and go, but she always gave the hardest time to Sam because she liked her. She remembered when Sam first came to "her" ER: bright, spirited, and ready to take on the world. Wendella saw the passage of time and the perennial shortsightedness of the administration wear down even Sam's solar energy. Wendella spent many quiet shifts with Sam, listening to Sam's ideas for how to make life better for the patients and staff. That's all Wendella could do was listen because she knew no one in administration would. She looked much younger than her fifty-four years and six children she raised as a single mom. She always said that African American women aged well. All those kids kept her in shape, despite her mommy-roll under her scrub pants.

"Dr. Sam, when are you going to learn how to write legibly, girl. I swear I'm gonna start a scholarship fund to send you to penmanship school."

Wendella grabbed her cane and made her way to the copy machine room. She tried not to bear any weight on her left knee, which just had replacement surgery. Sam told her to take more time off, but Wendella laughed.

"Wendella, you know what a challenge my life is. I'm just trying to share the joy."

Wendella peered at Sam over her parochial black glasses.

"Thank you for sharing." She marched herself back to the reception desk and put the cane next to her. She thought it might actually come in handy with all the nuts that wandered into the ER.

"Now, if you are no longer in need of my fine services, ma'am…" Sam removed her white coat and hung it up in the back lounge, just over her cherished, worn stethoscope. "I'm off shift and off to a movie."

Wendella straightened up in her chair hoping for the answer she was searching for from Sam.

"Please humor me, and tell me you're actually going out on a date."

Sam shook her head from side to side, and restrained a laugh. "Sorry, ma'am, not your lucky day."

Wendella's response could be heard over the patient in the next bay screaming for a bedpan. "Quit callin' me ma'am before I slap you, child. Lord knows I wish you'd get lucky."

"Oh yeah, my last date, I don't remember much. I was so tired I fell face first into a plate of spaghetti." Sam slid her arm into her down parka and started her escape down the hall. "He took me home real fast."

Wendella handed Sam a fax before she was able to make a getaway.

"Almost forgot, Medical Staff Services sent down this memo. You have three charts to complete by midnight or you're suspended."

"I see our Medical Staff Services coordinator hasn't lost her touch." Sam took off her coat and draped it over her arm.

"I think her recent boob job is squeezing all her skin too tight; now her two brain cells are battling for space up there."

Sam made her way into the dictating carousel in the lounge behind the ER reception desk and settled her coat on her lap. She dialed Nin's cell phone.

Nin couldn't decide between the traditional pumps and the pointy-toed, high-heeled hooker shoes. She gleamed at the shoe salesman. She picked up her cell phone after waving the salesman to wrap up the hooker shoes.

"Hey, Dr. Sam, you ready?"

"I just got socked with three discharge summaries." Sam propped her feet up on the ER lounge table.

"Relax, lady, I still have our key from when I housesat last year, and besides, there's a late show. I'll head over to your place and meet you there."

"I won't be long, Nin. I promise, no 'War and Peace.' 'Bye." Sam threw the three charts on the table and grabbed the dictating machine.

SAM'S APARTMENT BUILDING

Nin was a little slower tonight getting to Sam's apartment. The slippery terrain of the wet street was a challenge for her new hooker shoes. She made it up the steps of the building, but took off her shoes when she got to the scratchy red carpet in front of Sam's apartment. She kept trying to get the door open, but the key just wouldn't turn. Tommy walked out of his apartment and remembered Nin from her frequent visits during the summer months. He liked it better when the weather was warm and she came over in her halter tops.

"Can I help you, miss?"

Nin dropped the key on the hardwood between the red carpet and the door. She turned around to see it was Tommy.

"I can't seem to get the key to work."

Tommy leaned over and into Nin while he picked up the key. "Let me help. Dr. Sam seems to have problems with it, too."

"Oh." Nin stood sandwiched between the door and Tommy.

"I watch her sometimes when she gets back from work." Tommy put his hand over Nin's hand and jiggled the key in the lock. He turned the key without much effort and the door opened. He waited to release Nin's hand.

"Sometimes you just have to get it in the right spot, and apply a certain amount of force. It'll give in."

Nin smiled and stuck the key in her coat pocket.

"Really? Thank you. I'll remember that for next time."

Tommy walked toward his apartment then turned to face Nin.

"I'm always here."

Nin went into the apartment while Tommy stood outside the door and waited. He heard the deadbolt turn from inside.

Nin shivered from a blast of cold air when she walked into Sam's apartment. She could almost see her breath. Sam usually kept her apartment warm, almost steamy, like a deserted tropical island. Tonight felt different. Nin turned on the shower a little extra hot to make up for the coolness in the apartment air. She took off her clothes and quickly got in when she was startled by a noise in the hallway.

"Sam, back so soon? I bet those discharge summaries are one line each," she yelled, over the water heating up every inch of her frozen body. She closed her eyes and turned her head from side to side toward the shower head and let the soothing stream run down the length of her body.

The light went out in Sam's window. Sam was racing up the street to her building, but she didn't notice it go off. She was more concerned about grabbing Nin and getting to the movie on time. A challenge for both of them. Sam unlocked her apartment door and felt a whiff of steam and hot air when she entered her front hallway. She heard the water rushing in the shower. Nin was notorious for her long, hot showers to the point of setting off the fire alarm one too many times.

"Nin, why are all the lights off in here—you got a surprise for me?" Sam hung her coat on the antique coat rack in the foyer and started walking toward the bathroom, then slowed down her step. She wasn't sure who she would find with Nin in the shower. It had happened before, which is why she and Nin always got along so well. Sisters from different mothers they called each other.

"He better be worth looking at, or he's not coming with us." Sam pulled her keychain with Pete's photo out of the garbage before she got to the bathroom door.

"You sure are taking a long shower in there. Is he in there with you?" Sam couldn't take the suspense of Nin's mystery man, and thought what the hey as she opened the bathroom door in slow motion.

Sam lost all color in her face. She saw Nin's legs hanging over the edge of the tub, covered in blood. The water from the

45

shower created a river of red on the tile floor. She screamed uncontrollably, especially when she saw the words, "Next time" written in blood on the mirror.

LEAVING

Ralph leaned forward in his chair with both hands gripping his desk. Sam's thumb started to bleed from all the skin she had picked around the base of her nail. He'd seen that many times before. She couldn't stop her knee from shaking and her foot from incessantly tapping the carpet.

"It's not the same now, Sam." Ralph stared at the raw edges of Sam's thumb. She folded her hands in her lap. She could never hide her nervous habit from Ralph.

"I know. I have to do this now, Ralph, or I'll never get out of here and God knows what could happen then. I have to leave, at least for a while."

Ralph stood up and started walking over to Sam. What once was Ralph's confident protégé had been replaced by a woman who couldn't even decide what to eat on the menu anymore.

"I've already called Ray Connelly, Sam. He knows the whole story and has assured me you will be protected. Those loggers may not be your kind of people, but they're going to make sure you don't get dead."

Ralph picked up a manila envelope off his desk and opened Sam's hands, placing the envelope firmly in her grasp, "Ray has you scheduled for patients already this Monday. We've sealed your medical staff file, and I'm telling everyone you're going back to the Midwest for a brief leave of absence to be with family. No one but me will know you are in Alaska at the logging camp."

The manila envelope felt like a lead weight in Sam's hands. Every step toward the door felt like one more step further away from the life she had known, not a great or inspiring life, but a known life. She turned and faced Ralph, silent for once.

"Ralph, anyone else would've given up on me in this place after my first bender."

The sides of Ralph's lips rose to a comforting smile.

"Even geniuses struggle with demons, Sam. While you're gone, take care of that demon. It makes you the fighter that you are."

Sam shut the door behind her. Not a loud slam, like Ralph was used to, but a quiet locking of the door. It's as if she hadn't been there.

Ralph opened the file on his desk marked "Dr. Samantha Nolan/Confidential." He ripped off the sheet of paper at the top labeled "Temporary Assignment to Woodbridge, Alaska." Only the staples from the sheet were left behind. He folded up the paper and put it in his coat pocket.

PETE

There seemed to be more traffic in the police station than usual for late morning. The night shift cops, hookers, and everyone else generally were gone by now. Sam was glad that no one noticed her come in. She wanted to stay quiet, along with the reason she was there. O'Brien never missed Sam in a crowd.

"He's been waiting for you all morning, Sam." O'Brien tilted his head toward Pete, who was sipping his Tully's coffee while reviewing his last write-up. Pete couldn't lower himself to drink Starbucks, that was for the guys on the beat.

Sam sat in the chair next to Pete's paper-strewn desk.

"You okay, Sam?" Pete put down his coffee and stopped everything he was doing. These were the only moments he could savor with Sam.

"Not really, but I'll fake it." Sam played with the zipper on her handbag. Time with Pete moved in slow motion. She kept pulling a strand of hair off her face, but it wouldn't stay back. Pete pushed the stray into her dark locks. She could smell the nicotine on his fingertips, heavier than usual. More cigarettes meant there was more going on in Pete's life.

"There's nothing fake about you, Sam." Pete leaned as far forward in his chair toward Sam as he could. Sam handed a folded slip of paper to him.

"Here's where I'll be for the next six weeks. Can you pick up my mail?"

"Sure." Pete was curious and opened up the note, which he quickly scanned. "Alaska? You're not serious. I hear it gets pretty cold up there. But then again, it can get pretty cold down here too."

Sam got up from her seat and buttoned her coat. Against her better judgment, she looked directly at Pete.

"I guess I deserve that one."

O'Brien was watching them as they looked at each other. He knew that look, he had seen it and lived it with them before. O.B. motioned Garren Taylor over to his desk. Garren's towering, thin frame gave away that he had once been a star forward with the University of North Carolina basketball team. His Versace suits and Bruno Magli shoes fit right into his new city lifestyle.

"Sam, I want you to meet Detective Garren Taylor. He's looking into your case."

"Nice to meet you, Dr. Nolan. Can I spend a few minutes with you to go over some details before you leave?" Garren stood at attention, waiting.

"Sure." Sam nodded to Garren.

"Take care, Sam; you know how to reach us," O'Brien reassured Sam. Sam reached over and hugged O.B. with a daughterly embrace.

"Thanks, O.B." She clung to the safety of O'Brien's shoulders a little longer than usual. Pete stood still while Sam and O'Brien embraced. He wanted it to be him. Sam waved goodbye to Pete. O'Brien started back to his desk, but not before he noticed from the corner of his eye that Pete was watching Sam walk away.

WOODBRIDGE, ALASKA

Sam rolled down the window of her BMW so she could get a better look at just how green the trees were that were hovering over her car. She should've gone with the all-wheel drive Subaru when she thought about navigating these winding roads with a blanket of snow. But would she really have to be here that long? Around the last turn she saw her immediate future, "Welcome to Woodbridge, AK, pop. 730." Sam pulled to the side of the road and slammed on the brakes. She rested her forehead on the steering wheel. *My God*, she thought, *where has my life gone?*

The mountainside was sparse with loggers today. Just a sprinkling of flannel shirts and suspenders, instead of the usual patchwork pattern. Skye counted only eight of the usual fifteen of his crew having shown up. Ron could see the blood rising in Skye's veins, which Skye tried and always failed to conceal. Ron was the second oldest member of the Woodbridge Logging Company, next to Ray Connelly. Ron remembered Skye's first day on the job. Ron had his silver hair and beer gut back then, but he never felt passed over by Ray for putting Skye in charge. Ron, like everyone else, knew how Skye's star shone in Ray's eyes and no one ever resented Skye for it.

"Where the hell is everyone, Ron?" Skye looked around the empty worksite.

"You're the hooktender, Skye. I don't keep track of 'em."

Ron yelled to Jack above the noise of the chainsaws. Jack

yelled back from over the brush he was clearing, "I think a bunch of the guys went to see the new doctor we got in town."

"Doctor! How come my slinger and chokerman heard about this new doctor before me?" Ron and Jack clammed shut when they heard Skye's tone of voice.

"I want to meet this new doctor and the first thing I'm going to do when I see him is wring his neck. Half my crew's in his office." Ron and Jack gave their best poker faces to Skye, and their best smiles to each other.

"You should definitely go down there right now, Skye, and meet this new doctor." Ron kept himself from letting out a gut-busting laugh.

"Yep," Jack chimed in, "definitely."

THE CLINIC

Millie Connelly, Ray's wife, had been the medical clinic's receptionist before it was even built eleven years ago. Millie had seen several doctors come and go. Woodbridge just didn't appeal to the big city types: no symphony, ballet, or opera, not even a movie house. The bowling alley just didn't do it for them. Even the locals got sick and tired of the same music in there all the time.

Skye stormed into the clinic after wiping his boots off at the door. No matter how angry he was, Millie's wrath against any logger who muddied up the waiting room carpet was no match.

"Skye Ronan, what in the world brings you in here like a tornado?"

Skye glanced around the waiting room filled with his loggers.

"Millie, your husband owns this logging company, but he made me the hooktender to run it. How can I run a logging company when half the loggers in this town are sitting in here reading Family Circle? They can't all be sick at the same time."

Skye stared at Butch, one of his young, buff loggers. Butch put down the Family Circle magazine on the pine coffee table in front of him. Millie's reception room, as she called it, had manners and rules.

"Mornin', Skye." Butch pushed the magazine away from him farther onto the table. Bill, Butch's partner in crime, shoved the GQ behind him against the back of his chair, then straightened up his back.

"We're just here to see the new doctor, Skye." Butch let out his breath, and the GQ fell to the ground.

"All of you? At once? Will someone please tell me what is so great about this new doctor?" Skye stood, waiting for an answer.

All the loggers looked at each other and smiled. Millie knew it was her time to cut in.

"Go in, Skye, it's just Ray with the doc in there..." Millie waved Skye on in.

He knew his way around the back of the office. He'd been in it many times with loggers with broken bones, head injuries, pneumonia, even appendicitis. He looked for the green flag above the chart file slot outside the exam room door. That meant there was a patient inside with the doc.

Skye started opening the door to the exam room. Millie decided to finish her sentence then and called back to Skye, "…gettin' his hemorrhoids checked out."

Skye walked into the exam room with a picture perfect view of Ray's butt hole and Sam's back to Skye.

Skye, looking away, said, "Jesus, Ray, Millie said I could come in."

"It's okay, Skye. Meet our new doctor, Samantha Nolan. Dr. Nolan, meet Skye Ronan."

Sam turned around and Skye definitely noticed she was a female.

"I'd shake hands, but I'm all gloved up and this glove's been somewhere already today."

"Sorry, ma'am, they didn't tell me we were getting a girl, I mean a female, actually I mean a woman doctor."

"No problem, Skye. Dr. Sam here didn't know she was getting a grouchy hooktender to deal with." Ray, off the table by now, started pulling up his pants.

"Yes, sir." Skye stood frozen.

"You wanted a doctor so bad, Skye, and I was able to corral Dr. Sam. You don't want me to send her back now, do you?"

Skye started shaking his head from side to side and just kept shaking it.

"No, definitely, no."

Ray stood by the door and faced them both. "She's all yours, Skye. You wanted to tell her something?"

Ray exited the room, but left the door open a crack, so all

the loggers in the waiting room could gracefully peer in. By now, they had huddled outside the hallway entry to try and hear what was going on, worse than a bunch of Gossip Girls.

"Was there something you wanted to discuss with me, Mr. Ronan?" Sam threw her gloves in the garbage and waited patiently for an answer from Skye.

"I...I need some new safety guidelines for the chokerman."

"Ray did say safety was an issue for you." Sam put one hand on her hip.

"He did?" Skye looked surprised.

"I brought some manuals with me; they're at my cabin."

"Okay." He couldn't help but stare at her lips. Then he wondered if she caught him staring.

"That means I don't have them here," she explained.

Skye brought himself back down to earth.

"Yeah, right, I'll get them later," he replied.

Skye walked out to the hallway and looked from side to side. Sam could tell he needed some help.

"Nice to meet you, Skye, and the waiting room is back that way."

He wasn't paying attention too well at this point and didn't hear the scurrying of feet back into seats in the reception area. Skye passed by all the loggers in the waiting room and quickly got back into his zone.

"Each of you gets five minutes in there with her, then I want all of you back to work."

Butch leaned over to Bill. "That's cuz Skye wants her for five hours."

Millie waved Skye on to the front door of the clinic.

"Later, Skye. I'll try to get Field and Stream for the office so you can feel better."

THE CABIN

Sam slowed her mind long enough to hear the wind traveling through the thick branches of the trees outside her living room window. Then there was a silence that seemed to last for hours. If she wanted peace and quiet away from the hospital and the frenzy she'd left behind, along with Pete, she got it. She pulled a photo of her and Nin out of the last box she was unpacking and placed it on the table next to the front door.

It looked like it was going to take weeks to clean up the last person's mess.

Millie and Ray loved this cabin. It had been in their family for years. Usually they were very strict when they rented the cabin, but it was hard to be strict with Ray's sister. The only time she got off the couch was to get more food out of the refrigerator. Millie finally fixed that problem, and found her a job in Juneau. Ray owned the logging company, but Millie ran the show. Thank God, Sam thought.

Sam heard tires rolling up in the gravel driveway from the kitchen. By the time she got to the front door, she could see Skye's outline through the curtained window in the door thanks to a little light from the late afternoon sun. She opened the door before he could knock.

"Oh, am I catching you at a bad time, Dr. Nolan?" Skye wiped the sweat from his brow, and it seemed to drip all the way down his arms and legs to his mud-soaked work boots. Still breathing hard from a day on the mountain, it made him shine that much more in the day's last vestiges of sunlight.

"No, come on in. I just finished getting settled." She led the way.

Skye wiped his boots off on the old, bristled scraper outside the doorway. One good habit ingrained in any self-respecting logger.

"So that's what it's for," Sam commented as she shut the door behind Skye.

"Sorry about my appearance, Dr. Nolan. I came straight from the mountain here to pick up the safety manuals."

Sam couldn't help but stare at Skye's biceps after a hard day's worth of work. She quickly looked away before Skye could catch her staring. She picked up the safety manuals from the dining room table and gave them to Skye.

"It's...Sam, call me Sam. It's only when I'm in trouble some-one calls me Dr. Nolan."

"Is trouble your friend or your enemy?" Skye wiped his brow on his shirtsleeve. He couldn't resist the opportunity to catch her off guard. He caught Sam fidgeting with her hair.

"I never thought of it either way," she replied, keeping her hands down at her side in an effort to hide her anxiety. Skye didn't walk too far into the house.

"I've learned to make friends with trouble over the years.

Woodbridge is a great place to do that." Skye saw the photo of Sam and Nin.

"Is this your sister?" He sensed she seemed uncomfortable with all his questions.

"Sort of, a good friend...she died recently." Sam's frown was all too apparent.

"Is that why you're here?"

"I guess I'll find out why I'm here in the next few weeks, won't I?" Sam answered carefully, and she wondered how much Skye actually knew.

Skye watched Sam roll up her sleeves so she could really get down to cleaning the cabin. Skinny arms, he noticed—typical city girl. Woodbridge would change that.

"I gotta go. Can I take you up the mountain tomorrow so you know what you're in for?" Skye started out the front door.

"It's a date," Sam said and quickly added, "I mean I'll meet you up there tomorrow."

Skye turned to face Sam and gave her a grin through his workingman's stubble.

"That it is then." He made his way back to his truck with a smile on his face, knowing she couldn't see it.

NIGHT

Sam curled up in bed with Larry McMurtry's *Lonesome Dove*. Having displaced herself to Woodbridge, she felt she should get to know the Wild West. In her case, it had become the Wild Northwest Territories and beyond. No matter how much she turned up the heat on her electric blanket, she just couldn't get warm. Millie and Ray never had a chance to insulate the cabin properly but they didn't expect anyone to actually live in it for longer than two weeks at a time.

Sam wasn't sure how long it would take for things to die down at home. When it came to Pete, though, things never died down. She knew she had to call him sooner or later. She picked up the phone and dialed.

"Pete, it's Sam."

"Sam! Everything okay?" Pete woke up from his first REM stage.

"I'm fine. How's the investigation going?" she asked.

He sat up on the side of the bed and reached for the clock. Midnight. She always was a night owl.

"No leads. Taylor's had all dead ends. Say, I picked up your mail and a letter came with no return address."

Sam's hand shook as she tried to take a sip of tea from the cup next to her bed on the night table. Pete could hear it clang against the saucer even through the phone.

"Open it, what does it say. Is it signed?" Sam spilled the tea all over her night table, until it was dripping on the hardwood floor.

"No, it's blank. Hey, isn't Father's Day in—"

"—June. Thanks, Pete, I'll get back to you." Click.

Just another typical call from Sam. Pete placed the Father's Day card on his bedside table, next to the photo of him and Sam embracing.

THE MOUNTAINSIDE

Sam got halfway up the hill toward Skye before she ran out of breath. She realized that she hadn't been keeping up with her exercise these past few months and it was starting to show itself. Not so for Skye. Skye fit the image of the quintessential logger. Big, sweaty, and surrounded by trees and logging equipment. She wondered if she would be able to keep up with him, on the hillside that was.

"Good morning, gentlemen." Sam tried to hide her curiosity about Skye and the other loggers. They all stopped in their tracks to gaze at Sam, then picked up the pace after Skye flashed one of his infamous "start movin' your ass again" looks.

"Hey, Dr. Sam, thanks for the medicine, my shoulder feels better already." Butch waved to Sam as he called out from across the field.

"You're welcome, Butch. That's what I'm here for."

Sleeter Vandovich couldn't help but notice Sam. His 6'5" frame towered over the other loggers. He wore a deep scar over his left eyebrow like a badge of honor, and he had plenty of other unseen scars from all the bar fights he'd been in since he was sixteen years old. Some of the fights had included Skye over the years. He resented Skye for getting the hooktender job he'd boasted would be his. Ray Connelly knew Sleeter would be a barking dog to the other loggers. All that hate and anger had to go somewhere. Sleeter broke from his conversation and walked over to Sam. Skye positioned himself in front of the doctor.

"Get back to work, Sleeter. You and Jack need to check the chains on your forklift. I think there's a problem."

Sleeter took one step closer to Skye. "I don't see a problem, Skye. Do you, Jack?"

Skye curled down his lip as Jack motioned to him. Jack didn't feel like breaking up a fight this early in the morning. Skye picked up a sledgehammer off the ground.

"Yeah, I think there's a problem, Sleeter, go check it anyway." Skye clenched the hammer even harder. Sleeter threw his pickaxe over his shoulder.

"Nice meetin' you, ma'am. I'll see you around."

Skye waited for Sleeter to walk down the hill. He never turned his back to Sleeter. He picked up a hard hat off the ground and gave it to Sam.

"Does this mean I get the tour now?" Sam kept turning the hat around to figure out where to stick it on her head.

Skye tucked Sam's deep brown hair under the hat. He could smell her lavender shampoo on the tips of his fingers.

"It isn't pretty, but you gotta wear it…regulations."

Skye started up the mountainside and reached out for Sam's hand before he would go any further. "Come on, take my hand."

Sam stopped walking. "What do you mean?" She took a step away from Skye.

"Come on, take my hand. I'm not going to risk you falling off this mountain on your first time up here. Do you think I'm crazy to take that risk? Let's go, I don't have all day."

Sam reached forward with slow indifference toward Skye, and before she could take a deep breath, he reached past her halfway and grabbed her hand, pulling her up the hillside. The light broke through the trees and her face felt warm from the sun, surrounded by the cooling air from the higher elevation.

Sam couldn't believe all the detail and mechanics that went into logging a hillside. The loggers were weighted down with safety equipment and spoke their own language. They looked like soldiers ready to go into battle; steel-tipped boots covered in mud and grass, red suspenders holding up their worn denim jeans, carved into their frames from years of work and sweat, and helmets with safety glasses to protect their faces from the splattering debris in the forest. There was so much noise and activity, Sam wondered how Skye, or anyone else, could keep any signals or orders straight. Skye spewed directions to everyone and never missed a beat. He made sure today that he didn't miss Sam's attention. She was a captive audience, he knew it, and he wasn't going to lose this window of opportunity.

"When do they say 'timber'?" Sam pointed to two guys pulling on a chain that was about to lower a tree.

"When they want to act like real loggers." Skye smiled.

Skye walked Sam over to the transport area where they hauled the trees down the mountainside and back into town. Like ants on a hill, everyone had his job. The jokes were abundant, although a little cleaner today. Sam overheard two loggers laughing about a prostitute and her dog, until Skye showed up. Skye looked at the loggers, then at Sam, then back at the loggers.

"We're almost done, Skye," they said as they waved.

"Yes, you are," Skye yelled back.

Sam watched the processor, which seemed bigger than a

battleship, trim the branches off the trees. The grinder was even noisier, and shaved the tree into what would eventually be the everyday lumber everyone knows.

They ended up in Ray's office, just in time for Millie to walk in. Millie used her authoritarian voice to get Skye's attention.

"Now, Skye, don't bore this poor woman. She'll want to leave and we just got her here."

"Hey, girlfriend, come over here and give your old man a hug." Ray still had it for Millie after all these years. She was the only one he would see in a room.

Millie and Ray hugged and kissed a little longer than Skye and Sam felt comfortable with. Skye crossed his arms in front and Sam took a step away from Skye. Millie grabbed her handbag before Ray could catch her again.

"Skye, I'm gonna have to steal Dr. Sam away from you early. I'm taking her to the Wagon Wheel."

"I forgot about the Wagon Wheel, Dr. Sam, but I knew Millie wouldn't," Ray said. He walked over and sat down behind his desk, to feign he was busy.

Skye made a beeline for the door. "If you're taking her to the Wagon Wheel, Millie, then she's all yours."

"What's the Wagon Wheel?" Sam furrowed her brow.

The room went quiet with blank stares.

THE TOWN

Sam looked out at the audience. The mean age of the room was about seventy-three. She liked everyone's hairstyle, though. Big hair and purple-tinged perms never seemed to have left Woodbridge. Millie stepped up to the microphone. The closer she got, the louder the obligatory screech of the electronics filled the stage. Some of the women reset their hearing aids accordingly.

"May I have everyone's attention? That means you, too, Shirley."

Millie allowed enough time and patience for Shirley. Shirley loved to wear her mint green wool dress to the Wagon Wheel. She was convinced there was a draft in the room and it made her feel warmer, in spite of the pink and gray slippers she wore to every meeting. No one noticed them anymore. The gray was just the dirt that had built up over the years, but everyone figured at eighty-two years old, let the woman have dirty slippers, she's earned them.

Even with her hearing aids, Shirley missed half of what was said to her. Her osteoporosis made her walk with her cane, which she shook frequently at the teenagers in line at the grocery store when they tried to move her along too quickly. Millie thought the fact that she had to hunch down lower than everyone made her miss a lot of conversations. Conversations in Woodbridge she probably didn't want to hear anyway.

"My pension? Hank never left me a pension, Gladys, what's

she trying to tell me?" Millie asked of the woman sitting next to her.

Gladys herself was pushing seventy-five. Everyone thought her wheelbarrow figure was the reason she was voted as president of the Wagon Wheel so many times. Gladys's husband, Lou, wanted fresh bread baked for dinner every night. He said the warm aroma of the blended sweet flour reminded him of coming home from school. He never knew that Gladys baked two loaves every afternoon and had already finished one before he even walked in the house.

"No, she said attention, Shirley, not 'pension.' Just sit down. We're about to start."

"Okay, okay, you kids." Shirley swatted her hand in frustration and plopped into her seat.

Millie beamed like a proud peacock. "Today is a very special day for Woodbridge, as I am so thrilled to present to our Wagon Wheel someone we have all been waiting for, for a long time. Ray was finally able to find her for our community. Let's give a warm Wagon Wheel welcome to Dr. Samantha Nolan, our new doctor."

The girlish excitement filled the air like a roomful of geriatric cheerleaders. Sam was used to jeers from her hospital administration and male colleagues. She kept looking to the back of the room, waiting for a tomato to be flung in her face.

Shirley tried to adjust her hearing aid and leaned over to Mabel, her seatmate. "A new hooker? Why does this town need a new hooker? We already have—"

Mabel pushed up the bottom of her Playtex bra so she

could breathe. "Dammit, Shirley, she said 'doctor,' she's our new doctor."

"Mabel, you mean she's a hooker who became a doctor?"

Frieda was the only one of the group who at eighty had kept her figure. Her tall, Norwegian frame towered over all the osteoporosis-challenged women of the group.

"Gladys, will you take Shirley to get her ears cleaned out by the doctor. I hate it when she gets this way."

Frieda had been a schoolteacher for over forty years. She could keep a group quiet, no matter what their age.

Sam kept a safe distance from the microphone. She didn't want to hear any dogs howl if she spoke too closely and set off the banshee sound from the microphone.

"I really don't know what to say. I feel so privileged that you invited me to this community." She stood deadpan, staring into the gray-haired field of the masses.

Blanche Mason was the local funeral director's wife, but she was not without a sense of humor, although unbeknownst to her. Her soft, Gibson-girl bun and square-framed glasses highlighted a much younger looking face than seventy-two. Blanche raised her hand.

"Yes, Blanche, go ahead. Do you have a question for the doctor?" Millie braced herself.

"Dr. Nolan, I'm Blanche Mason and wish to welcome you to our community. Will you only be treating the working loggers, or will you also be treating the retirees too?"

Millie tapped her finger on her other hand, waiting for the other shoe to drop.

"I believe I'm here for everyone." Sam gave Blanche a reassuring smile, but she was careful not to tell how long she would be there for everyone. She didn't want to put a damper on their excitement so early in her stay.

Millie closed her eyes, hoping her ears would follow suit. It was coming.

"My husband, Norman, is a retired logger. Do you know anything about the new thirty-six-hour Viagra—does it really work?"

"Oh…Yes, that's called Cialis." Sam looked at Millie, pleading for a road to follow. Blanche turned to address her dear constituents, who never tired of Blanche's entertainment.

"I hear if your husband takes it Friday evening, he'll have an erection all weekend. Is that true, or is that just something they say?"

Millie stepped to the microphone and motioned Sam to sit down.

"Blanche, why don't you have a seat, dear. This is exactly something you and Norman can take up with the doctor in her office." Millie firmed her voice. "In private, Blanche."

Shirley cocked her head to the side and leaned over to Frieda.

"Election? Is it time to vote for mayor again?"

"No, Shirley, she said erection, not election." Frieda screamed into what whisper thin remnant remained of Shirley's eardrum.

"Blanche, are you trying to kill Norman? He just had a heart attack last year," Mabel reminded Blanche.

"Mabel, I didn't know Norman farts a lot—can the new doctor take care of that?" Shirley wasn't about to back down and definitely wanted to stay part of the action.

"It's a 'heart attack,' a heart attack, Shirley." Mabel threw up her arms.

"Dr. Nolan, we really are glad you're here and we really do want to welcome you. In our own way," Gladys said.

"I can see that." Sam smiled.

"I think it's time for lunch." Millie wiped her brow and tried to redirect.

JAMIE

Jamie had been working at the Rooster Café since she was sixteen years old. How quickly twelve years had raced through her life. She thought she would be in Nashville making her fortune by now, but life had intervened. After her father died, there was no one to take care of her mother, stricken with multiple sclerosis. They couldn't afford an aide, and someone had to run the café. It was only logical that Jamie take over. She never held it against her mother, as long as she got to sing to someone, even if it only meant singing to the customers. They actually seemed to like it, making her even more endearing to them.

Millie and Sam sat at the counter in the back, hoping not to be seen by any of the ladies from the police auxiliary. It was donation time.

"Say hello to our new doctor, Dr. Samantha Nolan," Millie called over to Jamie.

Jamie set her coffee pot on the worn linoleum counter and wiped her hands on her peach and pear printed apron. She had worn that same apron nearly every day, the same one her mother wore all those years she worked the café when Jamie was growing up. Laden with coffee and grease stains that could never quite be washed away, it reminded her of all the friends and townspeople who'd made a special effort to eat at the café, just to keep their family afloat.

"It's about time this town got a sense of reason. We've been waiting for you for a long time." Jamie gave Sam a strong handshake, a working woman's handshake.

"So I notice." Sam liked her already.

"I mean it, maybe we can figure out a way you can put Prozac in the water supply. I must serve a thousand cups of coffee a day around here to treat everybody's depression. I nearly run out of coffee before the end of the week."

"I don't think that'll even get everyone thinkin' straight around here." Millie surveyed the crowd to see if anyone was listening.

"Woodbridge sure isn't what I expected." Sam sipped her coffee, then dowsed it with sugar and cream. It was a far cry from the gourmet brands she was used to at home. Millie and Jamie gave each other a sigh of relief. When your town doctor hits the sugar and fat-laden creamer, you know things are going to be good.

"These are good fellas up here, Dr. Sam. While you're here, you're part of the Woodbridge family now." Jamie waved to the customers who had just set off the jingling bells of the door to the restaurant.

Millie slapped Dr. Sam on the back.

"I signed you up for the sewing circle. Next meetin' is Sunday. Gotta go, Frank Mitchell's Hereford's just about to drop a new calf."

Millie put a few dollars on the table and left the café. Sam put her cup out to Jamie for a refill.

"What's next, church?"

Jamie poured from a fresh pot into Sam's cup. The steaming aroma reminded Sam of her many two a.m. nights in the ER. Somehow, she longed for them again.

"Services are at nine a.m. on Sunday. If you don't have a Bible, Dr. Sam, you can borrow one of mine."

Sam spilled the coffee all over Jamie's freshly cleaned counter. "Thanks."

THE CLINIC

Sam had quit wearing her white coat years ago. The reflex hammer and ophthalmoscope, along with the tongue blades, prescription pad, and tuning fork tugged on her swan-like neck to the point where she ended up looking like a hunched-over goose instead. It was a good thing that she got relocated to Woodbridge. Her jeans and fleece vests made her fade into the local scenery. She took the chart out of the pocket outside the exam room door and flipped through it. After she opened the door of the exam room, the gentleman inside stood up and at attention.

Hmm, must've been in the military, only those guys will stand up for me, she thought. "Good morning, Mr. Fetter. Please sit down."

"Call me Butch, ma'am." Oh God, that word again, 'ma'am.' Sam rolled her eyes out of Mr. Fetter's glance. I must be a million years old. Sam sat on the stool in front of the exam table. This was going to take a while.

"Okay, Butch. It says here you have a personal matter you want to talk about with me."

"Yeah," Butch whispered under his breath. Sam could hardly hear his response.

Sam leaned forward and softened her voice.

"It's okay, Butch, you can talk to me about anything. Are you…okay?" Sam looked over her eyeglasses. "You know—okay?" Butch straightened up in his chair.

"Huh? Oh no, no Doc, my frog's jumpin' fine. It's about Elva."

"Go on." Sam nodded attentively.

Butch put his head in his hands and let out a big, slow sigh. "See, Doc, a couple years ago Elva got real sick, and she almost died. I had to take her to Juneau for a big operation. Next week is her fiftieth birthday, and I really want to do something special for her."

70

Sam didn't realize she would have such a severe crisis on her hands, but was she up to it?

"I don't know how I can help you with that. I'm a doctor, Butch."

"I can't talk to anyone around here, they've known me since I was shootin' my BB gun from the back of my dad's pickup truck. I thought about gettin' her a bow and arrow, but that doesn't seem very romantic...What do you think?" Butch shook his head in despair.

Sam put down her chart on the exam table and leaned back. She hesitated, in deep thought.

"Sometimes, Butch, it's the littlest, least expected things, at those rare moments that are the most precious of all. What does she like?"

"She likes the new Westinghouse stove I bought for her."

"I bet if you took that stove, cooked her a gourmet dinner, set a beautiful table with a bundle of red roses on top and fed her dark chocolate all night long, she'd never forget that birthday."

Sam grinned with complete pride in her proposed solution. Even Sam felt surprised that she'd come up with such a romantic idea, knowing what a bonehead she was about relationships. Not bad.

"Wow, and I'd be right there enjoying it with her." Butch's eyes lit up the room.

"Yes, you would, Butch." Sam winked and added, "And it'll just be the two of you." Sam's first crisis at her new job and she'd sailed right through it. She hadn't lost her touch.

"Thanks, Dr. Sam. I know what I have to do." Butch raced

out the exam room to the front desk, where he found Millie filing charts.

"Millie, I feel better already. Thank Ray for bringin' her here."

Millie closed the door to the filing cabinet. She affirmed, "I will," then turned to see Sam join her behind the counter, munching on the white peppermints with the little green centers in the candy dish at the reception desk.

Millie cocked her head to the side. Sam handed Butch's chart over to Millie.

"What'd you do to him?"

"It's the bedside manner."

THE COMMUNITY CENTER

The sewing circle met every Sunday evening. It was the only time all week the women could get away from dinners, dishes, laundry, mopping and various other Woodbridge domestic activities. How did anyone over the age of eighteen survive in this town? The circles were split into neat and tidy groups: the big hair girls, the spinsters, the widows, the weight challenged, and the orphaned. If you didn't fit into any of the categories, but you didn't want to feel left out, you went into the orphan circle. This week it consisted of Sam, Jamie, Mabel, and Millie, among others.

"Ouch, these needles hurt!" Sam squeezed the blood out of the tip of her finger and sucked it up between her lips. Jamie kept going and didn't drop a stitch. She'd been there before.

"Dr. Sam, I hope you gave yourself a tetanus shot before you came tonight. Looks like you're gonna need one if you're gonna be a Woodbridge girl."

"Oh, Jamie, stop it—you remember how hard it was when you first got started." Mabel still refused to let her optometrist prescribe non-visible bifocals into her glasses. She was old and proud and wanted everyone else to know it.

Millie checked her stitches for their neatness and orderliness. The patchwork of yellows, reds, greens, and black made no sense to her close up, but when she stood back and took in her efforts, the picture that lay before her seemed to put itself together into a beautiful mosaic.

"What did you decide to work on, Dr. Sam?"

Sam stared at her audience like a fifth grader called on in class to show her artwork. She only hoped this wouldn't be a tougher crowd than the fifth graders. The suspense drove through every vertebrae of her spinal column until she took a deep breath and held up her needlepoint.

No one spoke. Sam exhaled. Their faces said it all. Millie decided to take a guess. She squinted and leaned forward. "Is that a deer on a tree stump?"

"It's a cow dancing in the forest," Sam replied.

Jamie nodded her head from side to side. She could accept that. "I see it's something you can always remember us by when you get back home."

"By the way, Sam, where is home?" Mabel placed her needlepoint in her lap, waiting for an answer.

"That's right, Dr. Sam, we never did get where you're from." Jamie stopped sewing too.

"It's like you showed up out of nowhere and poof," Mabel flicked her hands up in the air, "you're here with us now."

Sam started tugging at her needlepoint and couldn't get the thread to pass through the linen obstacle. Millie reached over and steadied Sam's shaking hand, so no one else could see. She gently untangled the different colors for Sam.

"Dr. Sam, you wanna come over to the buffet table and help me get some punch and brownies for the girls?" Shirley was as deaf as a doornail, but her brownies screamed chocolate.

"Right there, Shirley." Millie retreated with Sam to the food, while Mabel and Jamie hesitated to resume their work. Mabel leaned over to Jamie.

"What's that all about?"

"Got me, it must be something they don't want us to know about."

Jamie tightened her linen and ran her fingers over the perfect stitches. Out of the corner of her eye she caught Millie and Sam whispering on the way to the kitchen.

Millie kept loading more and more brownies onto the serving plate, then shoved it toward Sam.

"Here, take these, I'll go back over and change the subject."

Sam tried to find an open spot on the buffet table, but it was already filled with every kind of sugar product known to humankind.

Miranda Lakeland was getting bigger and bigger by the day. Some women say during their pregnancy they can feel their baby kick. For Miranda, her baby was kickboxing and turning somersaults at the same time. Through much effort, she made her way over to Sam.

"Dr. Nolan?" Miranda asked in a gentle voice.

"Yes, I'm Dr. Nolan."

Miranda reached her delicate hand out to Sam. "I really want to thank you for agreeing to come to Woodbridge."

Sam raised the plate of brownies up to her chest. "Sorry, I'd shake your hand but I'm all sugar and chocolate right now."

"That's okay. I feel like if we had you sooner, my Adam would be here today."

Sam absorbed every syllable of Miranda's sweet voice. "Your Adam?"

"Yes, my husband's name is, rather was, Adam. He died in a logging accident before you got here."

Sam lowered the plate of brownies so they weren't blocking Miranda anymore. "I am so sorry."

Miranda rubbed her belly. "Little Jake, or Josie, will never meet their dad, but I just hope you're here when this baby's ready to come out."

"Hopefully, I'll be right here to help you." Sam's face relaxed.

Miranda pulled out a beautiful brooch from her pocket. She rubbed the raised cameo carving between her fingers. She liked to feel the strength and softness of the coral.

"I really want you to have this, Dr. Nolan. Adam gave it to

me and I feel like his death helped us finally bring a doctor to our town."

"No, I just couldn't." Sam tried to turn.

Miranda stood in front of Sam, placed the brooch in Sam's jacket pocket, and zipped it tight. "You're part of our lives now and we're grateful to you. You're a real member of this community."

The plate of brownies felt heavy. Sam put them down on the buffet table.

RALPH PEYTON'S OFFICE

The flashlight showed the desktop marker: "Dr. Ralph Peyton." The black-gloved fingers rummaged through the papers covering the patient files below. The drawers opened slowly so as not to give away the intruder's presence with an untimely squeak. The flashlight made its way to the bookshelves against the wall and stumbled upon a file sticking out on its end that read "Dr. Samantha Nolan." The outside was marked Confidential. The intruder placed the file on the desk and started scanning the papers inside. There was one document that stood out in bold letters marked TEMPORARY RE-ASSIGNMENT. The intruder's fingers traced down the document to the part that read "Temporarily released to…" then a blank. The name and address were blacked out with a marker. The intruder grabbed the file, but knew better than to throw it against the wall.

RAY AND MILLIE'S HOUSE

Ray, Millie, and Skye sat waiting at the dinner table. Skye had been to their house hundreds of times before, but it had not looked like this. Millie's lace tablecloth, fine china, and sterling silver foretold a special occasion. The daisies with baby's breath graced the center of the table. Skye had been bringing them to Millie, her favorites, since he was sixteen years old. He thought his serious façade would hide his curiosity. He thought wrong. Millie knew Skye. The table looked like a perfect photo in a gourmet magazine, except for its lack of food and three very hungry people.

The front door absorbed the shock of a heavy knock. Sam was still out of breath by the time Millie opened it.

"I'm so sorry about being late, I just couldn't get away from Shirley when I met her in town this afternoon."

"Honey, the energizer bunny couldn't get away from Shirley." Millie took Sam's jacket.

Sam walked into the dining room and stopped before she got to her seat when she saw Skye. He pulled her chair out for her.

"Isn't it always like a doctor to be late," he said with a smile.

"Come on in, Sam; we weren't going to break our small town manners and start without you." Ray waved Sam over.

The warm, thick steam from the vegetables, baked potatoes, and garlic chicken filled the room with relaxing aromas. Everyone could take a deep breath now. Millie took her place at the table and reached out her hands.

"Come on, Sam, you too. I don't know about you, but I need all the prayin' I can get."

Skye gladly accepted Millie's hand, a Sunday dinner ritual for him. He reached out to Sam. Sam heard every tick of the clock go by, then she felt her hand settle into Skye's soothing grasp. Everyone bowed their heads to Ray's deep voice.

"Bless us, dear Lord, and this generous bounty that you have bestowed upon us. May we be worthy of the strength and grace you bring us. We are most grateful that you have brought Sam into our lives."

Ray smiled at Millie from the corner of his eye. Skye forgot himself in the moment and couldn't look away from Sam.

"And may we give back to her even more than she gives to Woodbridge." Ray noticed Skye finally came out of his trance.

"Amen." Millie concealed her high hopes.

Ray let out a big belly laugh as Skye tried to entertain Sam with their logging stories. He figured since she hadn't been to Woodbridge before, he could say anything and she wouldn't know the difference. Millie was trying to count if this was the one hundredth time she had heard this story. Skye flailed his arms around the corners of the table.

"So Ray says to me, 'Get your ass up that tree, Skye, or you'll be wearing those chains around your ankles.'"

"I shouldda taken myself up on that offer when I thought of it. You've been givin' me lip ever since." Ray cracked a smile while he shook his head at Skye.

"I still think the skunk in the outhouse is my favorite, Skye," Millie blurted out while she started taking the dishes. Sam widened her eyes for this story. Least to say, she was intrigued by it all.

"Can you believe it, Sam? Skye tells me the health inspector was in earlier that day and said he'd shut me down if I didn't fix the outhouse. I walk in there, Skye locks me in until I promise to give everybody a thirty-pound turkey for Thanksgiving."

"Just takin' care of my men, boss."

Millie had most of the dinner table cleared when she headed into the kitchen. Everyone at the table could hear the clang of the dishes and water running in the sink. Ray kept chatting it up.

"I think the Saran Wrap on the toilet seat—"

"Ray, get in here and help me!" Ray turned and saw Millie use her head to wave him toward her and away from Sam and Skye.

"I better get in there. You two go sit on the porch. We'll call you for dessert. Go ahead."

There wasn't a cloud in the sky and the stars looked like silver dots on a midnight blue blanket of velvet. The dogs were barking their own special language in the distance. Sam settled into the wicker rocker, which creaked with the rhythm of her motion. Skye leaned against the porch banister. That was the best place on the porch to get a full view of Sam.

"Ray and Millie are the best thing that's ever happened to me." Ray lowered his eyes.

"Yeah, why's that?" Sam slowed down the rocker.

"I lost my mom real young."

"What about your dad?" Sam seemed curious.

Skye paused. "Let's just say he wasn't around much after that."

Sam didn't push it. "I'm sorry."

Skye crossed his arms. "I'm not. Ray and Millie helped my grandparents whenever they could. Ray and Millie raised me like they raised their own two kids. They knew how hard it was for my grandparents to have an eight-year-old suddenly join their home later in life. Ray made sure I finished high school, even sent me to trade school before he would give me a job with the company."

Sam slowed her rocking chair to the beat of a pendulum on a grandfather clock. "Must be nice to have someone who cared so much about you and wanted you to succeed."

"Look what you've accomplished. Your parents raised a doctor. They probably were shootin' moonbeams from their chest on your graduation day from medical school."

"Mom beamed, Dad didn't quite make it there. Hangovers can be vicious." She raised a half smile.

"What about you?" Skye blurted out.

"What do you mean?"

Skye stepped closer to Sam. "What's the best thing that's ever happened to you?"

Sam's rocking motion came to a screeching halt.

Millie opened the screen door. "Are you two ready out there?" Sam and Skye stood motionless, looking at Millie.

"For dessert?"

THE CLINIC

Fridays were hectic for Millie, even in a small town clinic. The office was filled with people who wanted to get prescriptions filled before the weekend, the phone wouldn't stop ringing, the single moms with bladder infections couldn't keep their kids quiet, the mail hadn't been opened yet, and this was all before Millie had a chance to put on a pot of coffee.

The front door of the clinic burst open. Jack and Bill rushed Skye into the waiting room with blood dripping on the carpet from the gauze wrapped around his right upper arm. Millie almost dropped the phone out of her hand.

"I gotta go. We have an emergency." Millie started yelling before she could get to Skye. "Dr. Sam, get out here right away."

Sam ran out of the exam room with her stethoscope still hanging off her neck. "What is it—what happened?"

Jack lifted Skye's upper body. "Skye's always trying to do everything himself."

Bill tightened the tourniquet around Skye's arm. "One of the lines broke when we were trying to bring down a tree. Gouged his arm."

Sam peeled back the dressing to a bloody, zigzag laceration. Skye tried hard not to show Sam he was gritting his teeth.

"Bring him in the treatment room. Millie, get the suture set."

Skye took in a deep breath and the scent of alcohol filled his lungs. Why did hospitals and clinics have to have such white walls and empty comfort? Sam prepped and draped Skye's wound. She didn't know how much the regional anesthetic had kicked in, so she pulled a tongue blade out of one of the glass jars.

"Here, bite on this."

Skye tilted his head to one side. "What's that for?"

"I don't have any bullets for you to bite on."

"Just do it, Doc." Skye's face and T-shirt were covered in blood and sweat. He just wanted it done. Sam started suturing and could feel Skye staring, first at her eyes, then her nose and lips.

"Quit staring at me, it breaks my concentration."

"If I stare at you, it doesn't hurt as much."

Sam took another suture into Skye's arm, a big one this time.

"Ouch!" Skye tightened his right hand to keep from squirming.

"Told you, you should've taken the tongue depressor."

"I'll take my chances."

Skye fixed his gaze on Sam as she finished dressing the wound. He gripped the exam table with his muscular left arm and sat up.

"Keep it clean and dry for the next two days. I'm supposed to do a wound check in two days, but since it's Friday, I'll see you on Monday." The light knock on the door didn't give away who was there.

"Come on in, he's decent," Sam said with a laugh.

Ray eased the door open. He didn't know what he was going to find behind it.

"How's our patient? He gonna make it?"

Skye pointed his finger at Ray. "Ray, I'm gonna start

chargin' you combat pay." Skye raced past Ray and Sam into the waiting room. Sam started clearing off the gauze and needle from the tray table.

"He's fine Ray, but he sure likes to take risks."

"That depends on what kind of risks you mean. I don't think he takes them where he should." Ray leaned into the side of the doorway.

Sam waved him out, holding back a smile.

"It amazes me. How do you know so much about people?"

THE CHURCH

The white, steepled church lay against the canvas of an open field surrounded by sturdy evergreens. The voices from inside could be heard singing all the way down the road to the farthest cow pasture. Inside the church, Ray stood in front of the congregation with his arms extended.

"Good morning and welcome friends." Ray loved a packed house.

Jamie leaned over to Millie after she noticed Skye standing in the back of the church.

"Millie, that can't be Skye?"

Millie looked back to get a better view. "Watch your head, I expect the rafters will fall down any minute." The people in front turned and gave Millie and Jamie a perturbed look.

"What's he doing here?" Jamie whispered.

"He heard Dr. Sam was coming to church." Millie leaned into Jamie's ear.

"No kidding. Skye wouldn't even get out of his chair if Miss America walked in a room wearing a wet T-shirt." The people in front now motioned both to be quiet.

"Jamie, you're in church."

"I know. I'm a sinner, that's why I'm here."

Sam couldn't remember the last time she'd worn a dress. She was wearing the only one she brought with her to Woodbridge, and she was surprised she even had an occasion to wear it. She sat in the last pew. Years of Catholic school and churchgoing taught her how to position herself for a quick getaway. She didn't see Skye watching her from the corner of his eye on the opposite side of the church.

"There is nothing so blessed as a love between a man and a woman; pure, sacred, and untouched by the outside world." Ray caught Skye before he could look away. "For God said a man shall leave his mother, and cling to his wife."

Skye stayed behind in the church while the rest of the congregation wandered single file to greet Ray and Millie in the receiving line. Millie was surprised that she hadn't developed tendinitis yet with all the handshaking she'd done every week for the past twenty-five years. Sam was one of the last people to pass through the line.

"Is there anything you can't do, Ray?" Sam smiled.

"I can't practice medicine; that's why you're here."

Skye exited the back of the church, but couldn't help passing by Ray, Millie, and Sam. He took his time, deep in thought. Millie's gaze followed Skye's walk.

"And Lord knows, Ray, you couldn't cook a meal if your life depended on it," Millie said.

Sam turned to see Skye halfway to his truck. "I better check on Skye's wound." Sam hurried to catch up to him.

"What do you think, Ray, can she heal him?" Millie took Ray's hand in hers.

"I'm not sure who needs the healing here, Millie."

Skye heard the grass behind him rustle with movement.

"Skye! How are you?" Skye turned as Sam's pace slowed down to a comfortable distance.

"I'm good."

"Can I touch you?

"Huh?" Skye stopped.

"I mean, can I touch your wound?" Sam softened.

Skye pulled his arm in, guarding his dressing. "It's wrapped up pretty tight."

"Right. I'll be seeing it tomorrow anyway—the three-day wound check?"

Skye started getting into his truck. "Oh, yeah."

Sam picked at the skin around her fingers. "I'll be seeing you then, uh…your wound tomorrow, won't I? I mean if I see your wound then I'll be seeing—"

"I'll be there." Skye put the truck in gear and started driving away. Sam couldn't see his delayed smile.

Sam watched Skye's truck rumble down the dirt road into the blinding sun. There wasn't a cloud in the sky and the air was still.

"It's starting," she whispered to herself.

85

THE CLINIC

Skye was sitting in the waiting room when Pete walked in. Pete noticed Skye sitting alone, but didn't think much of it. He figured Sam was there to treat injured loggers, neurotic housewives, and fat-bellied old men with high blood pressure. A far cry from her ER days. Millie looked up from the disorganized day's schedule.

"Can I help you, sir?"

Pete flashed his badge at Millie. "Yes. I'm Detective Pete O'Halloran."

Millie braced her hands on her desk. "Oh no, did Daisy the cow storm the police station again? She must be hormonal."

Pete managed to crack a smile, against his better judgment. "No, ma'am, I'm here to see Dr. Samantha Nolan. Is she here?"

This caught Skye's attention. He stared at Pete's dark suit and polished brown leather shoes. What's a guy like this, without a flannel shirt or a baseball cap, doing up in Woodbridge and what did he want with Sam?

Millie got up and started heading to the exam rooms. "I'll see if she's available, Detective."

Pete looked around and stopped when he saw Skye's gaze fixed on him. An occupational hazard of a gumshoe. Millie made it back to the reception desk just in time. Two alpha males in one room, not a good blend.

"She just finished, Detective. I'll take you back."

Millie led Pete through the white hallways and past the photos of the old logging community.

The cabinets looked in good shape for vintage 1960s. Files were strewn everywhere and patient brochures overflowed the shelves. The more years that went by, the more the medical offices stayed the same. Sam closed the chart in front of her and looked up to see Pete.

"Pete! What are you doing here?"

Millie looked from side to side. Sam seemed more surprised than happy to see this guy. "So you two know each other?"

Sam stood there with her mouth open before she could get the words out.

"Yes, Millie. Pete is…a…with the police department that's looking into my case."

"Fine, then I'll leave you two alone." Millie took the chart from Sam and headed back toward the reception desk. They looked like they could use some private time.

"Thank you, ma'am," Pete called out.

Millie opened the door to the waiting room, enough for Pete to see Skye.

"Uh, Dr. Sam, Skye is in the waiting room to see you." Millie smiled at Pete, who was thin-lipped by now. "For that recheck on his wound."

"Right. I won't be long."

Pete put his arm on the wall next to Sam to make himself more comfortable, and to make sure he could be seen by Skye. "Good to see you, Sam. You look great. This Yukon country seems to agree with you."

Sam scratched the back of her neck. "Nice break from gunshot wounds. You came a long way, Pete—everything okay?" Pete even smelled the same. His aftershave never changed, no variety.

"I've got everything under control. Captain thought I needed a few days off, so he sent me up here to check on your case and take in the sights." Sam could see Pete sizing up Skye in the near-empty waiting room.

"You came at a good time. It's the Logger's Festival this week." Sam tried to change the subject.

Pete turned serious and pulled a card out from his coat pocket. He handed it over to Sam. She didn't want to, but she took it out of the envelope.

"This came to the station addressed to me." Pete lowered his voice.

On the front of the card was a plain, gray office building. Sam hesitated, then opened the card. The inscription read "Happy Holidays from your friends at Pacific Western Insurance Group." The handwritten message underneath read "I know you know where she is." Sam threw the card on the worn and stained carpet. Pete picked it up and rushed it into his pocket, but not before all the blood drained from Sam's face.

"This isn't making any sense. Father's Day cards in August, now a Christmas card out of season. What are they trying to say?"

Pete scratched his forehead and ran his fingers through his hair. The early gray was new. He hadn't had any when he and Sam were dating. Sam figured she must have been the source of that.

"Can you connect any of this? Do you have any friends or acquaintances who work there? What about any patients?"

Pete tried to give Sam the start of any leads in the case, but Sam drew a blank.

"It's a big employer in town, Pete. I couldn't keep track of everyone who may have worked there. Most of the time I don't even pay attention if a patient's employed, let alone where."

"I'll pass it along to Taylor, see what he can dig up." Pete sighed.

Sam watched the silence settle in between them. Some things never do change. Pete stared directly into her eyes, waiting for her to take the lead.

"How long are you here?" she finally asked.

"I leave day after tomorrow, with a stop in Juneau about another case on my way home."

Sam pulled her stethoscope out of the pocket of her white coat and wrapped it around her neck. The townspeople had bought her the white coat and had her name embroidered on it. They would give her anything if she'd just stay awhile. She rolled up her sleeves and started washing her hands in the nearby sink.

"I'm going to the Logger's Festival tomorrow. I hear the chainsaw contest is really incredible. Wanna join me before you leave?" Sam grabbed some paper towels and dried off.

"Sure," Pete answered, before Sam could change her mind.

Millie marched into the hallway with chart in hand. "Ready, Doc? I think Skye's anxious to see you."

"I better go." Pete cocked his head to one side, perturbed.

Millie walked Skye down the hallway toward the exam

room. Skye took his sweet time, especially when he came up to Sam.

Pete avoided Skye as he wandered toward the front of the clinic. He turned while he was still within Skye's earshot. "I'll see you tomorrow, Sam."

Skye came face to face with Sam. "Is it my turn now?"

THE LOGGER'S FESTIVAL

The Logger's Festival always raised the noise level in Woodbridge about ten notches. Every man, woman, and child in town never missed the three days of the smell of the popcorn, the sound of the cheering crowd, and the touch of pink candy cane sugar between the fingertips. They knew they had this only once a year, and no one was going to miss these memories for anything.

Sam and Pete emerged from the masses eating sauerkraut, relish, and hot-mustard-slathered bratwursts. Pete wiped some mustard off the side of Sam's mouth, while Skye watched them from across the square.

"What's a city girl like you doing in a place like this?" Pete wanted to know. Skye moved into the crowd.

"Sometimes a change of scenery can do a person good." Sam took the last bite of her brat and wiped her hands clean.

Skye's boots slapped the ground as he walked toward them.

He stood up straight and raised his shoulders. He wanted to give as much of a presence to Pete as he could.

"Makes you think about things in a whole new way," Sam said.

"Do you like what you see?" Pete hesitated. "The scenery, that is," he finished.

Skye had a nicer shirt on than usual, and even a pair of jeans that didn't have any holes in them. He stepped up his pace until he was standing between Sam and Pete. Skye focused more on Pete than Sam.

"Millie tells me you're up here on business," Skye said.

"Small town, Pete." Sam laughed, and added, "News travels at lightning speed."

Pete extended a handshake to Skye. "Nice to meet you too. I'm Detective Pete O'Halloran. A friend of Sam's."

Skye shook Pete's hand, but the wince he tried to hide came through. "Sorry, wound's still healing."

"Pete's here to…" Sam paused. "On some work for his department." Skye watched Sam twirl the ends of her hair, a dead giveaway.

"Woodbridge's a quiet place. Must've been an important reason to come all the way up here?" Skye inquired. The mid-day light showed off the red highlights in Sam's hair. Always a favorite of Pete's.

"I think so, and so does the department," Pete answered.

"Will you be leaving soon?" Skye placed his hands on his hips and spread out his stance.

"Pete's going back tomorrow, through Juneau," Sam jumped in.

"It's beautiful around here, but it's a little too chilly for my taste." Pete zipped up his jacket.

Skye raised a smile. He saw his chance, and on his turf. "We can't let you go back without experiencing our fine Alaskan hospitality first hand. I'd like to be the one to show it to you."

"Really?" Pete asked.

"What?" Sam worried.

"Not until I challenge you to a duel." Skye controlled his speech.

Pete pulled his hands out of his pockets and had both fists clenched behind his back. "What would we be fighting over?" Pete stayed clenched.

"Sam, you decide." Skye waited, then they both turned to face her.

Sam's eyes opened to the size of golf balls. A large gust of wind blew her hair off her face and left her porcelain skin bare and exposed. Skye started walking toward one of the game booths.

George Prescott was distinctly known around Woodbridge for his unflattering beer belly and the ever-present cigarette that hung out from the side of his mouth with an inch of ash that could fall off at any time. Besides being the only gun owner in town, he ran the best shooting booth at the Logger's Festival every year. George watched Skye stroll his way over. George knew the walk. He figured there must be a competitor around with that much of Skye's testosterone floating in the air.

"I figured I'd challenge you to something you know. George, give Detective O'Halloran here a weapon."

"No thanks, I've got one of my own." Pete flashed his holster. "Yep, it's the real thing. This is Alaska, isn't it? Even brought my own blanks George."

"Just don't shoot each other, I'm off duty." Sam decided she'd do best if she stood off to the side. George put out his cigarette and made sure he didn't blow any smoke in Sam's face.

"Each of you stay in your corridor. The deer will pop up, you shoot, most hits before the bell rings wins."

George rang the bell and the noise from one gun made Sam cover her ears. She held her grimace long enough to dull the sound of the second gun along with it. It seemed like the five minutes that wouldn't end. The shooting stopped, but the ringing in her head lingered. George put on his black, thick-rimmed glasses, which were held together across the bridge of his nose with duct tape.

"Let me count 'em. Skye, seventy-two. Detective, seventy-two. By God, you're even!" George pulled the target counter off the wall and gave them both to Sam. Skye tried, but he couldn't hold back his laugh.

"Will you look at that, we're exactly the same. Guess you have to pick the winner, Sam." Skye leaned against the counter and crossed his legs. Pete put his gun back in his holster and stood next to Skye.

"He's right, Sam. Which one of us is it going to be?" Pete loved putting her on the spot.

Sam pulled back her hair and twisted it into a bun on top of her head.

"I don't know. Do I have to choose?"

"Eventually everybody has to choose, Sam." Skye lifted the shotgun and handed it back to George.

Skye tightened the top button of his shirt and walked over

to get a hot dog. Pete threw a few dollars on the booth's counter and George stuck them in his shirt pocket.

"He's right, Sam, it's your call." George winked, out of Pete's sight.

THE LOG CABIN

The early morning sun squeezed through the front window of the log cabin. The porch light was still on from the previous night. A few sticks could be heard breaking off from the heaviness of the boots that were stepping on the ground in the nearby brush. A blue jay turned his head at the sound, then flew off. There was a perfect view of Sam getting ready for work, adding just that last touch of burgundy lipstick she was known for. Sam pulled on her beige raincoat and slammed the door shut behind her by kicking it with her foot. She looked up at a figure coming out of the brush.

"Pete, my God, you scared me."

"Why would I want to do anything like that to you, especially now?" He smiled.

"I don't want to be late to clinic."

"I came to say good-bye, I knew I'd miss you later," Pete said.

Sam pulled out her keys and started walking toward her car. Pete tried to keep his head down, but he couldn't stop looking at Sam. Her neck was always his favorite part of her, long, graceful, and comforting. He missed their better days. No matter where they were on earth, he was always saying good-bye to her. Sam stood outside her car facing Pete. It seemed like she was always saying good-bye to him, rarely hello.

"Thanks for coming up and keeping me informed. I'm sorry I can't help you with any of these clues."

Her voice softened. She felt like she had let Pete down in some way.

"Not your fault. My job's to figure this out, to get into the mind of this person who is so obsessed with you that you're all he can think about, all day, every day, every hour, every minute," he said.

Sam took a step back from Pete. His eyes looked different to her—sunken, dark, and withdrawn. She'd never seen him like this before.

"How'd you think someone gets this way, Pete?"

"It's easy, just take a good look at yourself."

Pete kicked a tree branch out of the way and took one step toward Sam. He leaned against the driver's side door with his arm up, hovering over her.

"You're right. I do need to take a good look at myself. Maybe there are some clues I've been missing." Sam clicked the car door lock open. "You better go; you've got a long trip home."

"Enjoy the rest of your stay here, Sam. I'll be waiting for you when you get back."

Pete wandered back to his car, calling to Sam over his

shoulder. Sam held her hand firmly on the driver's side door handle. She wanted to see Pete leave before she did. She thought she'd locked all the cabin doors before she left, but couldn't remember. Pete got into his car and started it up. He lowered his window so he could have a few more seconds with Sam.

"Sam, one last thing."

"What?"

"Tell Skye thanks. I always enjoy a challenge."

Pete's car dusted up the road with gravel and smoke. He turned the corner at the end of the field and fell from Sam's sight.

PETE'S APARTMENT

Pete's living room sought pride in its disarray. The police files of his cases from the precinct covered his grandmother's antique wooden table. Like a true cop, half-empty coffee cups highlighted nearly every room in the house. The intruder didn't feel like cleaning today. The photo of Pete with Sam took up the entire space on Pete's bedside table. The intruder picked it up and aimed at the floor, ready to smash it into a thousand pieces, then hesitated. Anything out of place always leaves clues. In the closet were squeezed uniforms, sweatpants, and an endless mass of dirty socks into every available space.

Their smell filled the intruder's lungs, who strained to hold a cough. Pete had tried to hide the gun he bought for Sam at Tumwell's shop, but it made it into the intruder's hands.

THE DANCE

Woodbridge's Paul Bunyan dance was always the highlight of the Logger's Festival. They held it at the community barn, a hundred-year-old donation from the Strickland family, the original founders of Woodbridge. Although it only came once a year, by the time Millie got through putting up the lights and decorating the tables with red-checked tablecloths, and the dancing started to Jamie's country twang, the whole town could be found under one roof.

"Sam, have we rubbed off on you yet?" Millie joked.

"I'm a little concerned...I watched a special on Patsy Cline last night on cable."

"Your cabin gets cable? You've got the luxury suite."

Ray's smile beamed brighter and brighter as he walked toward Millie. He extended his hand with a bow.

"I came to ask my lovely queen to dance."

"You people are so disgustingly in love," Sam said as she blushed. She noticed Skye walking in and she blushed even more.

Skye hadn't dressed up for any occasion in years. He didn't

think he would be able to find his high polished boots, let alone the crisp, white, button-down shirt Millie gave him for Christmas a few years back. He swore he'd die before wearing it. Millie eyed Sam watching Skye come in and leaned over to her.

"He cleans up pretty well, doesn't he? Your time is coming up sooner than you think."

Ray watched Skye head over to the buffet table. No self-respecting logger ever turned down a plate of food, whether or not he was hungry.

"What're you gonna to do then, Sam? Woodbridge is a small town," Ray said, while waving to Skye.

"There's no hiding here," Millie said, while following Ray's wave. Skye responded with a nod.

"Millie! Let's get out there before Jamie takes a break and someone from the high school puts on the rap music."

Millie and Ray escaped to the dance floor so as not to get cornered by the three musketeers: Frieda, Shirley, and Blanche, leaving Sam to fend for herself.

"Dr. Sam, we're so glad you're here in Woodbridge. Ernie's lumbago is finally cured," Frieda said. She put her last curl into place on her recently permed, purple hair.

"What, Frieda? Ernie's back on the rum again? I thought he quit that stuff." Shirley turned up the volume of her hearing aid.

"No, Shirley, it's time to change your hearing aid battery. Dr. Sam cured Ernie's lumbago," Blanche screamed over the music.

"I don't understand, why does Ernie want to go to Pago Pago? I thought he liked Woodbridge." Shirley removed her pink pointelle sweater. She had never got past the hot flashes of her menopause.

Skye leaned up against the beam post near the bar, trading jokes with Jack, Connor, and Matt. He let a laugh slip through and brushed his thick, dark hair over his head with his free hand, exposing his muscular arm through the white shirtsleeve.

"Now there's a reason to stay in Woodbridge," Blanche sighed.

"We've known Skye all these years. He's had chances with the most beautiful girls in and outside Woodbridge, but he just keeps…" Frieda struggled for the words.

"Waiting?" Sam finished.

"Commuting? Why would anyone commute to Woodbridge to work, half our stores are closed!" Shirley used her cane to steady herself and waited for someone to answer her.

Blanche grabbed Shirley's cane and took her by the arm. "Shirley, I'm taking you to the punch; yes, the rum punch."

Jack, Connor, and Matt could tell that Skye was losing interest in their conversation. He was interested in something, someone, else. Jack patted Skye on the back and waived Connor and Matt over to him and the dessert table. When Matt wouldn't stop talking Skye's ear off, Jack grabbed him by the arm and dragged him in front of the cherry cobbler. Sam couldn't see Skye walking toward her, but Frieda could.

"We used to be a big railroad town years ago Dr. Sam. That's how we got the name Woodbridge, for all the wooden bridges that were built for the railroad," Frieda said.

"I didn't know that." Sam sipped her cranberry punch and was careful not to spill it on her new floral shirt. Dark cranberry wouldn't blend with soft pink and blue cotton.

"Even now, you wait too long, you can miss your train. Hey, Skye," Frieda announced.

Sam turned and pulled her drink away from her face.

"Ms. Frieda, Dr. Sam." Skye nodded.

Skye hadn't looked this clean-shaven since Sam arrived in town. Frieda threw her shawl over her shoulder.

"I better help Blanche, or Shirley's gonna be swimming in rum punch."

Frieda ran over to Blanche, just in time to help her catch Shirley. Sam felt anything but alone.

"How's the arm?" she said.

"Almost completely healed," Skye replied.

"Great, guess you won't be needing my services anymore then?"

"That depends?" he asked.

Sam put her drink on a side table and sat down in the nearest chair. Skye took a seat next to her, then pulled his chair closer to hers.

"Depends?" she said, "I don't understand."

"You could help me—"

Sleeter came rushing into the conversation like an unwanted rainstorm.

"Evenin' Skye, Dr. Sam."

Sleeter stepped over near Sam, but didn't sit. Instead, he grabbed her by the arm and stood her up. "You're a city girl, come on, out on this dance floor and show me what you can do."

Skye leaned back in his chair and folded his arms across his chest.

"Can you handle what I dish out, Sleeter?" Sam said.

"I think you know a helluva lot more than what's in books."

Sleeter unbuttoned the top of his flannel shirt and tucked

his stringy blonde hair behind both ears. He pulled Sam toward his tanned chest, only to be stopped by her surprising strength. Sam's shoes squeaked across the dance floor as Sleeter rushed to center stage. He was always the biggest ham in the outfit. Her soft angora sweater fell off her shoulders onto the ground. Skye picked it up and folded it onto his chair.

Ray showed up and guzzled down the last of his dark beer. He smacked his lips to get rid of the aftertaste. Ray scratched his chin.

"You gonna go help her out? he asked.

"Something tells me she can take care of herself," Skye said.

Ray took the last bite out of Millie's best cherry cobbler. He savored the sugar against his lips and took a deep breath in to let its flavor linger for a while. Millie baked her cherry cobbler for the Logger's Festival and didn't make it much during the rest of the year. She knew Ray would appreciate her more if he wasn't getting it all the time. Ray wrapped his hand around the half frozen beer mug, which by now was dripping icy water onto his callused palm.

"You might be right, but I don't think she always wants to, Skye."

Sam looked over to see her angora sweater draped across the seat where Skye was sitting, and the back of Skye's leather jacket as he headed out the exit next to the blaring music of the band.

THE SEWING CIRCLE

Sam couldn't believe she let Jamie talk her into giving the sewing circle another try. She still felt the sting of the betadine against her raw skin from holes she poked into herself last time. The band-aids were still on, worn now with sweat under the adhesive. She didn't bother taking them off. She figured it would protect her from any more damage she'd do tonight.

Millie avoided needlepoint. The softer touch of yarn and crocheting was more her thing. She knew someone in town would eventually need something she made: a sweater, hat, scarf, or in this case, baby booties. Every baby in Woodbridge at one point in their life wore booties from Aunt Millie.

"You look like you're just ready to pop, Miranda."

"This baby's a kicker. He, or she, may make an early appearance." Miranda rubbed her gauze blouse over her belly.

Blanche took in the smell of the freshly baked bread from the back of the kitchen. The girls enjoyed watching the steam rise from the first slice and how smooth it tasted going down with unsalted butter and a glass of cold milk. This was the one night each week the girls treated themselves. All the husbands and boyfriends home with the kids, trying to stay sane amidst the diaper changing, piggyback rides and, oh yes, their favorite, bottle feeding.

"Sure glad you're here, Dr. Sam. We were afraid we'd have to deliver Miranda's baby all by ourselves," Blanche said.

"You're due in two months, Miranda. Dr. Sam will still be here and we won't have to worry," Frieda said.

Frieda heard the timer go off in the kitchen and put down her needlework. She raced off without waiting for a response from Sam. Millie cleared her throat and looked at Sam. No one else caught their glance. Jamie pushed the end of the knitting needle against her hip. She did her best by wearing a thick sweater over her middle to cushion herself from the cold steel.

"By the time I get Jack to ask me to marry him, I'll be ready to be a surrogate grandmother. Can you handle that, Dr. Sam?" Jamie asked.

Sam forced a smile without looking at anyone.

"I don't know what to say. I'll be...ow!" The sewing needle felt like an iron stake through Sam's finger. She squeezed the tip to force the blood out and dull the pain and throbbing.

The smell of fresh yeast grew closer and closer to the circle as Frieda arrived with the loaves of bread. Millie saw this as her chance.

"Here Sam, come with me. I think we have more band-aids in the kitchen. When Jamie told me you were coming tonight, I stocked up," Millie said.

Millie shut the brown revolving door to the kitchen behind her. She opened the glass cabinet overlying the tile countertop filled with cracks from many years of sewing circle gatherings. She pulled out the dusty box of band-aids from the bottom shelf. By this time, Sam had her finger under the rusty faucet, washing away the blood. She grimaced from the sting of the industrial bar soap against her bare skin.

"I haven't told them, Dr. Sam," Millie whispered.

"They think I'm staying here?" Sam asked.

Millie handed her a paper towel and Sam wrapped her

numb finger in it. She squeezed it tight until the bleeding stopped. Millie started removing the bread pans from the ovens and turned on the fans. She thought the lingering scent of fresh bread would help Sam calm down.

"Yes," Millie answered.

"Permanently?" Sam's voice jumped up an octave.

"We've waited for years, Dr. Sam, for a doctor in this town, and I just didn't have the heart—"

"What?" Sam wrapped the band-aid around her finger, but she made it too tight. Her fingertip was growing pale.

"You're not just hired help, Dr. Sam. You're one of us. You're part of our lives now. How can I say anything to them?" Millie asked.

"I'm no one special. I'm replaceable." Sam threw her arms up in the air. "That was the agreement I made with Ralph and your husband."

Millie took Sam's wounded finger into her hand and loosened the band-aid so the blood would return to the tip. She hung on to Sam's finger. She could feel it tremble against the rough edges of her own hand, which itself had known many years of indecision.

"Your head made that agreement, Dr. Sam, not your heart. What are you so afraid of?" Millie asked.

"Me, afraid? Look at my job. What do I do for a living? I'm not allowed to be afraid," Sam answered.

Millie put Sam's hand down on the countertop next to the sink. The laughter in the other room trickled across the revolving door. She threw a red-checked kitchen towel over her shoulder. The voices in the other room grew louder.

"Hear that? We care about you, Dr. Sam. We're part of your life now," Millie said.

"Millie, Dr. Sam, we need you two in here now!" the girls shouted.

"I'm going back in a few weeks," Sam replied.

"Your heart can't go back, Dr. Sam. Even you know that."

Millie swung open the revolving door and headed back to the sewing circle. Sam listened to the rhythmic sound of the door swaying back and forth between herself and the sewing circle in the next room over.

TOMMY'S APARTMENT

Tommy could taste the salt in his sweat dripping down the side of his face. He kept swallowing to keep his mouth from getting parched. Tommy's finger pressed and held the buttons on the telephone handset. He could hear the pulse tones in slow motion. Anything to stall.

"Dr. Peyton, please…thank you." Tommy's voice quivered. "Dr. Peyton, I've been trying to find a Dr. Samantha Nolan."

Ralph's voice hesitated on the other end of the phone.

"Dr. Nolan is on sabbatical right now and can't be reached. Who's calling please?"

"My father and her father worked together some years ago at the Pacific Western Insurance Group. He said it would mean a lot to him if I could find her."

Ralph sensed the missing information.

"She should be back at this hospital in a few weeks. Can you give me your name and next time I speak to her, I'll mention you."

Tommy rustled open the worn edges of the piece of paper in front of him with the words "Larry Dwyer" scribbled in pencil.

"So you're in contact with her?"

"I...can reach her. What is your father's name?"

"Dwyer, Larry Dwyer."

Tommy wiped the sweat from his brow. Ralph switched his phone to the other ear to give himself time to choose his words carefully.

"I have to be going, Mr. Dwyer. I'll let her know." Odd call, Ralph thought. How would anyone know to call him about Sam?

Tommy waited as long as he could to hang up the phone after the click. His knee couldn't stop shaking, which made his foot tap the hardwood floor.

"Was that okay?"

Tommy felt the icy sting of the gun barrel on his bare skinned temple. It was a perfect shot. His knee stopped tapping.

DR. RALPH PEYTON'S OFFICE

Ralph tried to focus on the medical journal. An article about oleic acid concentrations in diabetic mice didn't seem that exciting. The sound of the jackhammers adding the new hospital wing resonated through his office window. The concrete and rebar fumes finally got to him, so he closed the window. The jackhammer grew dull, but didn't go away. Ralph settled back in his chair and heard the squeak of the wheels after he leaned back and propped his feet up on his desk. He held the telephone receiver in one hand and the scrap of paper with the words "Larry Dwyer" written on it in the other.

"Sam, how's that icebox up there?" Ralph looked up to make sure his office door was closed.

"Ralph, let me go into my office." Sam put the call on park. "Millie, I'll take this in the back."

"Sure—everything okay?" Millie didn't like the sound of this.

Sam pushed open the door to her office. The smell of the lavender-scented candle she kept burning to help her relax filled the hallway with a light breeze when she shut the door behind her. Millie looked at the front desk phone and the blinking green light of the call on park steadied to a flat line.

"When can I come home, Ralph?" Sam paced the room.

"Ray tells me you're fitting in up there. What's the rush?"

"They think I belong up here."

"The question is, do you think you belong up there?"

Ralph used the scrap of paper to tap the marble clock adorning his desk.

"Do you know a Larry Dwyer, Sam?"

"Doesn't ring a bell; should I?"

"I got a call last night from some guy looking for you. Said he was Larry Dwyer's son, and this Larry Dwyer worked with your dad."

Ralph put his feet on the floor and leaned forward in his chair. Sam slowed down and took a seat at her desk.

"I never remember my dad mentioning the name."

"He wants to meet with you, like his father wants him to look you up. Said his dad and your dad worked at the Pacific Western Insurance Group together."

"I don't like this, Ralph. My dad never worked for an insurance company."

Sam tilted her head so she could rest the telephone on her shoulder and pick at the skin around her fingers.

"Quit pickin' at the skin around your finger," Ralph screamed into the receiver.

"Ralph!" Sam snapped, with real tension in her voice.

Ralph's mouth started watering when he realized his secretary had left a plate of oatmeal cookies on the table next to his desk. He couldn't wait and reached over for one.

"Listen, I'll take this Larry Dwyer thing to Detective Taylor who's investigating your case. In the meantime, have a little fun up there with the locals."

Sam noticed a photograph on the wall of Skye and Ray with a large Marlin they caught. It must've been some time ago, Ray didn't have any gray hair.

"I'm workin' on it, Ralph." Sam stuck her hand in her pocket so she wouldn't pick at her finger anymore.

"And do it sober." Ralph could barely get the words out from his cookie-filled mouth.

"All right, all right." Sam hung up and took a few minutes to stare at the photograph. Skye actually looked happy.

THE TAVERN

Fred Paxton had owned Woodbridge's oldest tavern, the Dark Horse, for over thirty years. After his logging accident, he and Ray played a lot of poker in the hospital while he was recuperating. The fifty pounds he originally lost became the seventy-five pounds he gained over the following year. His legs were still skinny, but he was grateful that his bar apron covered his well-endowed middle.

Lou Reilly used to own the bar, but lost it one night to Fred in a poker game. Fred says to this day that Lou did it on purpose. Lou left town soon after with a local girl half his age and Fred realized after Lou was too far away to track down, that the $120,000 bar debt had something to do with Lou losing his hand.

Fred was ecstatic when Sam came to town. He always thought that if Woodbridge had had a doctor when he got injured, he could've regained the use of his leg. Now he just told people it was an old war injury, and in a way, it was.

Sam sat alone wearing her brown leather bomber jacket to stay warm. She took a table close to the bar so she could talk to Fred and stay out of the cold draft that came into the bar every time the front door opened for another customer. Fred squeezed the dirty grey water out of the bar rag into the sink and scrubbed down the tabletops, yet again. Fred ran a tight ship, in and out of the bar.

"Dr. Sam, why don't I get you a Coke?" Fred threw the bar rag over his shoulder.

Sam stared at the shot of whiskey staring back at her. The pungent scent of the barrel-aged spirit couldn't reach her. She ran her finger over the top of the shot glass, deep enough for her to dip into its contents. The whiskey dripped off the end of her finger back into the glass.

"I just wanna sit, Fred." Sam propped her elbow on the table and slumped her face and chin into her right hand.

Fred stood over Sam with the Old Spice cologne trying to cover up the scent of his Skoal chewing tobacco.

"It's not worth it, Dr. Sam."

"What are you talking about, Fred?"

"I'm eighteen years sober." He leaned over.

"And you work in a tavern?"

"Work, hell, I own the place, girl." Fred shook his head. "But that's another story."

"Then who are you to talk?"

"I own it, so it doesn't own me. I never fear my demons, Dr. Sam. I love 'em, so I don't have to fear 'em."

Sam sat up to enjoy the aroma of the first few pizzas coming out of the brick-fired oven. She knew the place would be filling up soon. Between the pizza oven and new customers, the room was getting warmer. Sam took off her jacket. Maybe it was the conversation.

Fred took his place behind the bar and started filling up pitchers of beer. His customers got their money's worth, he kept down the foam. By this time, Butch, Bill, and Sleeter could be heard hollering over the classic country music spewing from the jukebox. Although Seattle was their closest major city in the lower forty-eight, the grunge music scene was a million miles away for these guys. You could hear the crack of billiards and pool cues, especially when it was Sleeter's turn. Skye came in through the back entrance and took a seat on his favorite bar stool with a perfect view of the HD TV. His hair was still wet. Fred wondered why Skye was in such a hurry to get here tonight, then he remembered Dr. Sam was sitting alone.

"A draft, Fred."

Skye reached for the bowl of peanuts and downed a handful. He rubbed his hands together to flake off the peanut skins while he scanned the room. By the time Sam looked up, Skye was standing in front of her.

"What d'you want?" Sam sat back in her chair after Skye took the empty chair at her table. He set his beer down in front of him and stared straight through Sam.

"Nothing, just thought I'd come over here so you didn't do anything stupid."

"What in the hell is that supposed to mean?"

Skye unzipped his nylon jacket and opened his top button. Sam continued to circle the top of her drink with her finger. Skye's rough-skinned hand took Sam's finger and pulled it away from the shot glass. He motored down the shot and chased it with his beer. Sam watched him smack his lips in satisfaction.

"Thanks a lot," she said, crossing her arms in disgust.

"Fred, Dr. Sam needs a Coke."

"Sure thing, Skye."

Fred brought the icy cold Coke to Dr. Sam and whisked away the shot glass. Sam tore off the paper at the end of the straw and blew it toward Skye. She hit him, even though he ducked.

"What's with you yahoos up here? Ray drags me to this godforsaken place to be your town doctor and you people spend more time trying to take care of me than I do taking care of all of you."

"Lord knows you need it."

"I don't need anyone to take care of me."

Skye squeezed his lemon into his beer. He leaned forward into Sam's face.

"Keep tellin' yourself that, maybe one of these days you'll believe it."

Butch, Bill, and Sleeter stumbled toward the front door. No one light a match thought Sam; she and Skye couldn't help but take in their fumes as they walked by.

"Hey, Skye, Dr. Sam." Bill was the only sober one so he had the car keys.

"Hail to the chief." Butch stood at attention in front of Skye.

Butch and Bill did their best to hold up Sleeter. His huge Norwegian frame was built for logging, like his ancestors before him. His family went as far back as the Gold Rush of 1896, but had lost their fortune in the stock market crash. Sleeter carried the family bitterness ever since. He never liked taking orders from anyone, especially Skye, the town's golden boy.

"I can't leave without getting one dance with my favorite doctor," Sleeter slurred.

"Sorry, Sleeter, I left my dancing shoes at home."

Sam took another sip until Sleeter knocked her Coke all over the table. He grabbed Sam by the arm and tried to pull her up.

"Come on, Sleeter, you're drunk." Butch caught the back

of Sleeter's red and black flannel shirt. Bill was heading for the door.

"Sleeter, leave it alone, Let's go," Bill said.

"We don't get city girls like you here that often, Doc. Just one dance before I go."

Sleeter tightened his grip on Sam. Skye moved his beer to the next table and stood up. Fred had seen this picture once too often in his tavern, to the tune of broken glass and thousands of dollars.

"She said no, Sleeter."

"We gotta put up with your hollerin' all day, Skye. This is our time and I'm gonna dance with the lovely doc."

Sleeter veered away from Butch and Bill. Skye grabbed the front of Sleeter's shirt and pulled him off Sam and into the bar rail. Sleeter made for an empty beer bottle and broke off the end, lunging toward Skye. Butch and Bill each took one of Sleeter's arms.

"Sleeter, that's enough!" Butch shouted.

"We're gettin' outta here now," Bill finished.

Bill dragged Sleeter out the front door. Skye started to clean off the spilt Coke with napkins when Sam joined him. She noticed for the first time all night that Skye was clean-shaven.

"Thanks." Her voice softened. "I guess I'm not as tough as I thought."

"I wouldn't go that far. Come on, let me walk you home," Skye offered.

Skye held Sam's coat while she tried to get it on. She was having trouble getting her arm in, so he gently picked up her arm and guided it into her coat sleeve. He zipped her jacket all the way to the top.

"It's cold out there; you'll need your body heat. Let's go."

Skye followed Sam out, while Fred wolfed down the last piece of pizza on the counter. He was just glad that he got through another night with his place not getting torn up.

THE CABIN

Sam and Skye could smell the cinders from the neighboring cabin's fireplace. They headed up the walkway toward Sam's front door where the porch light was on, attracting a group of moths hovering over the flame. Skye felt the same way. Sam turned to face him when she heard the owl in the large maple next to the house. Skye didn't even flinch, he was so used to it. The wind picked up and he could taste its cool breeze in the back of this throat. Sam stood on the top step and Skye was just one step below her, but his frame towered over her.

"I'm sorry I snapped at you back there," she said.

"You should know, I'm...we're really glad you came to town."

"Me too," Sam answered, just above a whisper.

Skye pulled his hands out of his jacket pockets, then lifted his right hand toward the left side of Sam's face. It looked so perfect and smooth. He stopped, and gently squeezed her upper arm through her coat. Sam glanced at Skye retreating his right hand back into his pocket.

A pair of eyes hid behind the machinery on the side of the cabin, waiting for Skye to leave. Skye watched Sam enter the cabin, then headed toward his truck. She turned on the dining room light, but raised her hand to her eyes to shield the light in the room. She used the dimmer to lower the light without ever seeing the face staring at her from outside the bay window.

The house was starting to smell like rotten fruit. She gathered up the trash in each room and threw it all into two large bags in the kitchen. Thank God, Millie was kind enough to leave her the heavy-duty bags, or she'd be cleaning up a huge mess off the floor. She grabbed the garbage bags and made her way to the dumpster next to the fence in the back yard. The screen door slammed shut behind her. Her shadow faded as she stepped away from the back porch light and got closer to the dumpster.

She heard a deep breath, not her own, then a large hand covered her mouth. She could smell the soot and traces of oil on the hands, a workingman's hands.

"I'm gonna get more from you tonight than just a dance, pretty doctor." Sam recognized Sleeter's voice. "Don't say a word, 'cause we're going back in the house for our own party."

Sam started biting Sleeter's hand. She heard another set of footsteps coming toward them, then felt Sleeter's weight loosening off her, like a backpack coming off her shoulders. She turned and Sleeter had Skye on the ground, kicking in his ribs. Sam tried to pull Sleeter off Skye but couldn't. Sleeter lost his balance, but not until he pushed Sam into the side of the dumpster and she cut her hand, struggling to stay up. Skye grabbed Sleeter by the throat and pinned him to the damp ground. He squeezed Sleeter's throat until he remembered himself.

"You lousy drunk, Sleeter. Get away from her and go home."

"Whatta you care, Skye, if she and I have a little fun. You might want her, Skye, but we both know you won't touch her, even if you want to, you won't. You can't make love to any woman, and you and I both know why."

Sleeter stood up and brushed himself off and wiped the blood from his lip. He started heading down the tree-covered path toward the center of town.

Sam cradled her hand. Skye could see her staring at him, Sleeter's words resonating in her head. He felt the tension in his ice-cold fist. Sleeter's laugh carried back into the yard.

"Get outta here, or I'll break your neck."

"Have fun with him, Doc, if you can," Sleeter shouted.

Skye waited until Sleeter was well into the forest and out of site. He checked Sam's hand, but couldn't look her in the eye. "Let's go in the house. I want to take care of this now," he said.

"Skip it, I'm fine. I can take care of it myself."

"I want to do this," he insisted.

Skye surrounded her wound with both of his hands and finally raised his eyes to meet Sam's gaze. They headed toward the kitchen and he locked the back door behind them, leaving the porch light on.

Skye ran the water in the bathroom for a few minutes while Sam kept her hand wrapped with an old, rough-edged towel. He tested the water, but could tell from the steam that it would be too hard on Sam's hand. He started to remove the towel and took his time. He didn't want to tear the wound any more than it already was. Sam inhaled a deep breath, then held it in to offset the pain. He cupped her hands in his and led her to the running water, immersing both their hands in the water until the towel drifted away and it was just their bare skin.

"What was he talking about back there?" Sam barely got her words out. She looked at Skye, watching his thick, black hair brush against the side of his face. He kept washing; he wouldn't look up.

"Sleeter's just drunk, small town, hard to keep secrets."

"What secrets?" Sam wouldn't let it go.

Skye opened the drain in the sink and the water swirled down into the rusty pipes. Sam used her free hand to raise his squared-off chin. He raced to smear the antibiotic ointment on her hand and wrap the dressing. After all the years on the mountain and treating injuries, he knew how to work fast. The medicine chest door squeaked and its mirror caught the light when he closed it.

"It's late, get some rest, you're workin' tomorrow. Someone's gotta take care of us yahoos."

THE POLICE STATION

Ralph didn't have a lot of time to spend at the police station. He had to get back to the hospital for rounds. He ran up the front steps and once inside headed straight for the reception desk. O'Brien pointed him toward Pete who was now filling up his Thermos under the cold spigot of the water cooler. He'd given up coffee thinking it would make him less irritable. It hadn't worked. Ralph was glad to find the right person right away, not an easy thing to do in this madhouse.

"Are you Officer O'Halloran?"

"Yes, sir. Can I help you?"

"I'm Dr. Ralph Peyton. Dr. Samantha Nolan told me to give you this information."

"Is she okay?"

"She's fine. I'm supposed to get hold of Detective Taylor. She said it's important to her case."

"Let me get him."

O'Brien took notice that Ralph was still out of breath. All he needed at seven o'clock in the morning was a heart attack in the precinct. He hated calling the EMTs. Their crew beat them at softball every year and they loved to rub it in every chance they got.

Pete gulped down his water then headed straight toward Taylor's cubicle. Ralph noticed Pete taking notes on a pad, until he broke his concentration long enough to tap Taylor on the shoulder and point to Ralph. Taylor nodded and they joined O'Brien and Ralph at the front desk. O'Brien, the runt of the litter, introduced Taylor.

"This is Detective Taylor. Garren, this is Dr. Ralph Peyton. He has information on Dr. Nolan's case."

Ralph and Taylor exchanged handshakes. A firm, tight grip. Must've been football in his younger days. Ralph stepped away from Pete.

"Can we go somewhere and talk?" asked Ralph.

"Sure," said Taylor.

Ralph scanned the room for a quiet place. Taylor waved Ralph to follow him. O'Brien headed back to his station with less redness in his face now. He tapped Pete on the shoulder.

"How's that serial rape case coming?"

"Slow. Any news on Sam's case?"

"Leave it, Pete, you're too close to this one. Taylor can handle it."

O'Brien pressed the volume button on his radio to turn down the incessant racket. Pete flipped through a file on the counter in front of him, only half reading it. He raised his hand to his forehead enough to hide his upward gaze toward Taylor and Ralph. Their conversation drifted into a muffle as Taylor shut the glass doors of the conference room.

THE CLINIC

Ray inhaled one of Millie's still warm chocolate walnut brownies. He pursed his lips to get the last of the lingering chocolate taste. She winked at him while finishing her phone call with an anxious patient. Ray leaned over and blew her a kiss. She laughed, hung up the phone and returned the gesture by planting a wet one on Ray's chocolate-covered lips, licking the last remnants of crumbs. Sam cleared her throat like a vacuum cleaner had just exploded in the waiting room.

"You want to borrow one of the exam rooms? I can go to lunch early."

"No thanks, Sam, we're slowing down in our old age. Now at least we wait until we get home."

"I'm actually here to see you." Ray smiled.

"I won't keep him long, Millie."

"I don't worry. I'm the one in charge of his Viagra."

Millie wiped the sides of her mouth with a Kleenex. She grabbed a patient file and started fanning herself. Within a few seconds her forehead beaded up with sweat and her face heated up to a hot poker. She'd never get used to these hot flashes.

Sam closed her office door behind her. She sipped her iced tea while Ray paced the other side of the room. Ray leaned against the side of Sam's desk. Sam tightened the gauze on her dressing. The rough edges tugged on the crusted blood of her injury, so she didn't pull it too tight. It hurt enough, but if it hadn't been for Skye, it would hurt more. Ray let out a sigh.

"Are you okay? Skye told me what happened."

"Skye did a great job fixing me up."

"I want to apologize about Sleeter. He hates Skye because I made Skye the hooktender instead of him."

"No problem, Ray. I'm just passing through. I'm only a visitor in Woodbridge."

"Yeah, yeah. I want to talk to you about that. We want you to stay, Dr. Sam, for good."

Ray stood frozen like a statue. The time it took for Sam's response felt like hours to Ray, but not to her.

"You've got to be kidding me. I don't fit up here."

"Who fits anywhere, Dr. Sam? You're here now, and we'll make it fit. Will you try?"

Ray took the reflex hammer off Sam's desk and started banging on his forearm. He moved it to banging on his head. With this conversation, a good place for it to be.

"You said 'we want you to stay.' Who's we?"

"Me, Millie, Ralph, the town."

Ray put down the reflex hammer and scratched the back of his neck before he looked up at Sam. He knew he had to get this out to seal the deal. Sam picked up the hammer and twirled it in her hand like a hummingbird flapping its wings. Why did everyone go to the reflex hammer to channel their anxiety?

"And Skye," Ray blurted.

"He told you that?"

"He tells me in his own ways."

"What ways?"

"My, the good doctor is just full of questions today, when I bring up Skye." Ray pulled the reflex hammer out of Sam's grip and lightly tapped her on the head with it. "You like a challenge. You figure it out."

Ray wrapped Millie in a bear hug on his way out front. She gently squeezed his arm as he gave her a slow peck on the cheek. Sam shook her head from side to side, only to look up and see Skye watching the same scene from her opposite view. Skye hadn't noticed her, so she slipped back to her office.

Ray grabbed a cherry flavored lollipop from the candy jar. He wrestled with the plastic wrapper, the sound crackling until they could hear the click when he popped it into his mouth.

Skye took off his cap and brushed his thick, coarse hair with his dusty hand. He threw his hat on the counter next to the candy jar.

"Speak of the devil. What're you doin' here, Skye? I don't pay you to go visitin' the women all day."

"Millie, are we up thirty percent in profits this year?"

"Ray, he's right."

Millie took a sip of her ice-cold lemonade and smacked her lips, refreshed. The little bits of sour pulp were the tastiest parts to her. There were certain days in life when a tart taste satisfied. Today, with Skye in his dry humor mode, was one of those days.

"All right, I trust your judgment," Ray relented.

"Good, now outta here. I'm here to see Doc," Skye said.

"You hurt again?" Ray braced himself for yet another work-related injury.

"I just came by to say thank you, my way."

"She's in back, Skye. Shut the door behind you." Millie winked.

"Wish I could be a fly on the wall for that meal," Ray said in a low voice as he leaned over to Millie.

Skye went to grab his cap, but decided to leave it on the counter. He headed toward Sam's office. The door was open and he could see her taking off her white coat and stretching to hang it on a wall hook. Skye didn't rush in. He enjoyed watching the outline of her slim figure.

He tapped lightly on the office door. "Hi."

Sam recognized his voice before she looked up. She realized Skye could see the blood rise to her face. He took a seat in front of her desk and stretched out his legs to get more comfortable. He didn't mind staying a while.

"How's your hand? Did I do okay?" He pointed to her dressing.

"You did fine, just fine."

"I'm really not here about your hand. Actually, I am, sort of. I'd like to take you to dinner, but not out to dinner, rather in to dinner."

"In to dinner?"

Sam furrowed her eyebrows with a half smile. She lit a vanilla candle on her desk, hoping the aroma would help calm her down. The flame's heat flickered upward and made her neck sweat even more.

"In my house. I'd like you to come over tomorrow night and I'll make you dinner, since you don't plan on stickin' around Woodbridge much longer. At least that's what I hear."

"Sort of like a last supper?" Sam removed the last remnants of her day by taking off her stethoscope and putting it in the desk drawer. She felt lighter already.

"In a way, I guess. That depends." Skye smiled.

"Depends on what?"

"That depends on how much you like the meal."

Sam threw her leather bag over her shoulder. The coolness of the hide brushed against the warm cotton of her dress. Skye took his time heading out with Sam to the front of the clinic. Mostly he just enjoyed any time he could he spend with her. Even if it was only watching her walk.

SKYE'S HOUSE

Sam was surprised how neat and orderly Skye kept the garden in front of his house. The azaleas and peonies were in full bloom, vying for the best colors on the lot. The wood carvings were all Skye, she thought, rough exterior with deeply imbedded inscriptions filled with meanings known only to him. She knocked on the door.

Skye threw a bunch of pots in the sink. He hurried to the living room to greet Sam with a cold bottle, dripping with ice.

"Come in, the door's open," he yelled, over the loud motion of the kitchen fan.

"Wow, I could smell this down the street."

"A person gets hungry loggin' all day. I figured years ago I needed a good, clean hobby, so I picked up cookin'."

Sam took off her coat and hung it on the oak coat rack Skye kept next to the hallway wardrobe. She admired his many fine antiques, adorned with intricate details and refinished to a glowing shine.

"Anything I can do to help?" She rolled up the sleeves of her cashmere sweater.

"You can pour the sparklin'…cider." He winked.

Skye handed her the icy cold bottle and she poured the cider into the freshly cleaned crystal wine glasses. The table linens looked European, white cotton with hand embroidered purple flowers, faithful even down to the mint green leaves. The red roses and baby's breath filled the air over the dining room table. There must have been two dozen packed into the cut glass vase.

"You know you can drink alcohol around me," Sam half-heartedly joked.

"I don't want to tempt you any more than you need to be tempted." He raised his glass. "To you, Sam. I hope you find what you are looking for, even if it's not in Woodbridge."

The high-pitched sound of their glasses toasting lingered in her ear. The cider went down Sam's throat cool and smooth, with an extra kick from the bubbles.

She never saw Skye move as fast as he did that night in the kitchen. She didn't say much at dinner, just listened as Skye laughed and told stories he couldn't tell on the job because they were all about the guys. She made sure to avoid any information about the hospital, what had been happening or why she was really there. The less Skye knew, the less chance anything would slip out to the others.

The blue-and-white checkered wallpaper in the kitchen looked brand new. Everything smelled of cinnamon, deep, fresh, and soothing. The bright red ladder-back chairs and country stove showed their age and usage. Skye started running the water in the sink. The steam rose up and frosted the window over the ledge above the sink followed by plenty of soap bubbles.

"At least let me do the dishes."

"Sure." Skye handed her the sponge.

"Just a second, pick up that towel and help me."

She started scrubbing but wouldn't let Skye make her do all the work. He grabbed one of his bar towels from the silver hook hanging off the cabinet next to the sink. This one was recently washed, dried, and fluffed. He hadn't known how observant of his housekeeping Sam would be so he tried to have everything clean before she got there.

"I'm not getting away from you that easy, huh?" Skye nodded.

The copper teakettle whistled and boiled over while Skye gently clanged the dishes putting them into the cupboards. Skye poured the hot water into their mugs, and instantly the room smelled of market spice. The sugar-laden shortbread cookies highlighted the tea flavor as they drank it.

"I hear tea is good for your heart; so I thought I'd give you some," he said.

"Tea, yes it's good for the heart; so is confession."

"What do you mean?" Skye asked.

He sat in the chair next to Sam and pulled it up to the table. Sam finished the last bite of her shortbread cookie. Skye leaned back in his chair. He shoved two large teaspoons of sugar into a fresh cup of tea and guzzled down his first sip.

"What's the family secret, Skye? What was Sleeter talking about the other day?"

Sam pressed the teabag between her thumb and spoon to squeeze the last of the spice out of the teabag.

Skye tapped the edge of his mug. "I told you my mom died and my dad was gone a lot after that."

"Yeah, and?" Sam leaned her arm on the table and rested her head in her hand.

Skye tightened the corner of his lip. He surrounded the mug with the calluses of his hands. He stiffened up and didn't feel the poker like heat of the cup against his skin.

"No, I just assumed there was more to it…" Sam trailed off.

"You're a doctor. You should know better than to assume."

Skye broke his shortbread cookie in half. The butter from the dough melted into his fingertips. He ate the half, lacing his lips with the white granules. The other half he lay next to his mug for later in the conversation. He began to stir the tea with his spoon.

"My father loved my mother so much, it killed them both."

"How's that?"

"When I was ten, Dad came home early from work one shift and found Mom with another logger. He ran the guy off, and beat Mom so hard he killed her. He died in prison."

Skye got up and threw the teabag in the garbage so hard he almost missed it. His mug banged against the ceramic sink. Skye ran the cold water to rinse the tea stain off his mug, but it wouldn't go away no matter how hard he scrubbed. He freshened Sam's cup with more hot water.

"I hope tea's good for your heart like you said. I could use it." Beads of sweat started to fill his forehead.

He gently wiped his dishes dry and put them in the glass cabinet with the others. Sam swirled her teabag around in her mug, until Skye replaced it with a new one. A fresh wave of market spice came over Sam again, and it seemed to calm down Skye.

"I'm so sorry you've had to live with this." Sam waited to sip the tea. It was too hot and intense.

"Millie and Ray made things safe for me again. I think that's why I'm afraid to…get too close to people. It kills you both; I couldn't live with that." Skye leaned up against the sink facing Sam with his arms crossed in front of his chest.

Sam felt a chill against her arms from the breeze coming in through Skye's back door. He noticed her rubbing her shoulders to create some heat. He put her hands in his and dropped her arms to both sides and lifted her up and out of her chair. She felt lighter than a feather, as Skye stroked both of her arms. She took Skye by the hand and walked him to the living room. She rummaged through the CD holder and found the one she thought would be just right for the occasion. The smooth, soft jazz weaved into the calming lights of the room.

Every inch of her graceful neck stood out to Skye. Her skin blended into the glow of the backdrop. Every step Skye took toward her felt an hour long. Her soft hands wrapped Skye's muscular arms around her waist. She cradled his neck and drew him closer to her. Skye could smell the jasmine in Sam's hand lotion as she gently closed his eyes and they both drifted off.

Sam's lips rested on Skye's as he brought her tighter to his chest. Her hair felt like silk: light, delicate, and endless. She stroked the leathery skin on the back of his neck. He wanted it that way.

THE CLINIC

Millie saw the blinking green light on her telephone and reluctantly read "11 messages" on the monitor. She tried to procrastinate by pulling charts for the next day before she took on the people of Woodbridge and all their complaints. With all the different colored charts: red, blue, purple, yellow, and scattered labels, she could do better than Shirley. Anybody could organize better than Shirley. Millie was already into the C's when Sam flew in.

"What d'ya think of Skye's venison stew?" Millie knew Sam's response wasn't going to be pretty.

"He fed me venison?"

"Relax, honey, it's hunting season. What didya think you were gonna eat?"

"My God, I've eaten Bambi!"

Millie lit the candle at her desk and the apple walnut scent reminded Sam of food. Not what she wanted to take in at the moment. She shook her head and slid off into her office, where she took a comfortable seat next to her desk and dialed the number. She picked up the receiver so she wouldn't be on speaker phone.

"Ralph, it's Sam."

"You sound great. What's going on up there?"

"If it's okay with you, I'd like to stay a little bit longer."

Sam fell silent, not knowing what kind of response she would get from Ralph. She knew from years under Ralph's tutelage that you never knew what you were going to get from him.

Ralph got up and carried the phone to the window to shut it. The constant jackhammering of the construction crew putting on the new wing of the hospital drowned out his conversation with Sam. This time he didn't want to miss a word.

Sam opened her office window to the sound of logs

grinding through the mill. She hadn't realized how much she had grown used to chainsaws splitting timber and the smell of fresh-cut evergreen branches.

The skin around her fingernail beds felt smooth and soft. The lavender mint healing cream Skye gave her kept its scent throughout the day.

"No problem. I take it you like Woodbridge?"

"Nice scenery. I've discover some interesting wildlife."

RALPH PEYTON'S OFFICE

Ralph's secretary squeezed through the door of his office far enough to let him know he had to hurry up his call. She kept his life easier with all the work she did to screen out angry administrators and money-grubbing vendors. He had learned to hang on her word.

"Dr. Peyton, you have another call on line two. He says it's personal and important."

Ralph nodded in reply.

"Sam, I gotta go. I've got another call coming in. I'm glad you finally stopped picking at the skin around your finger."

"Thanks, Ralph. Smart ass."

She heard his grinning laugh just before she hung up the receiver. Ralph pressed the bright yellow-orange blinking light of line two.

Ralph could hear the sounds of computer keyboards mixed in with screaming criminals and hearty laughter in the station background. O.B.'s precinct was one of the busiest in the city and by far the most colorful.

"This is Dr. Peyton speaking."

"Dr. Peyton, it's Detective Garren Taylor."

Taylor sipped the stale, cold coffee in the traditional precinct Styrofoam cup. What would a real cop do without his afternoon coffee leftover from the morning shift? Taylor cupped his open ear so he could hear himself talk into the phone. The vice squad had just busted a group of prostitutes and their shoes on the precinct floor sounded like a high school marching band.

"Garren! Any leads? I just got off the phone with Dr. Nolan."

"I found three Larry Dwyers," Taylor shouted into the phone. "Two of them went out of state over ten years ago, but this last one used to live in state. He died about two years ago."

"Anything worth chasing?" Ralph wrote the name Larry Dwyer on his desk pad with a big question mark next to it.

"Do you have access to all patient records?"

"Sure, as a physician I have unlimited access."

"Can you check the hospital medical records for a Lawrence Allen Dwyer, birthdate October 26, 1950?"

Ralph scribbled the information down. "Where are you going with this?"

"It's a long shot, but maybe if he was treated at your hospital, he's somehow connected to Dr. Nolan. Thanks, Dr. Peyton; it would help a lot."

"I've got a few minutes. I'll check it tonight."

Ralph tore the page with Dwyer's name from his memo pad and tucked it into the front pocket of his neatly pressed Van Heusen shirt.

MEDICAL RECORDS

Ralph headed down the hallway to the medical records department. The heels of his shoes clicked a brisk rhythm against the cold concrete of the basement floor. His shoulders shivered. Not his favorite part of the hospital. It always meant the bare landscape of paperwork.

When Victoria Sullivan worked the second shift, she brought a small ray of sunshine into the dark, quiet tomb. Every doctor in that hospital some time or another got to know Victoria. Having grown up in Catholic school, structure was her calling. Her filing system was lean, mean, and clean of any clutter.

"Good evening, Dr. Peyton. You're here late. Are you on suspension again for not finishing your medical records?"

"No, Victoria." He grinned over his wire-rimmed glasses. "Have we ever treated a Larry Dwyer, birthdate October 26, 1950?"

Victoria sped her fingers across the computer keyboard like playing the piano and punched out the demographic sheet onto her industrial strength printer. Ralph's eyes widened through his chiseled lenses, hoping to get some element of a clue to this whole mess. She rustled through the bundle of papers with her classic rapid pace.

"Lawrence Allen Dwyer, October 26, 1950? Looks like he never got past the ER."

"Who was the emergency room attending physician the night he came in?"

"The only name listed for the physician is Dr. Nolan."

"Thanks, Victoria. Can you get me the chart?"

"Sure, Dr. Peyton; it was less than two years ago so it hasn't been archived yet."

Victoria sifted through the miles of charts. She could hear Ralph tapping the counter with his increasing crescendo, a regular sign that he was on the move and so should she be.

Ralph could get back to his office with his eyes closed. He flipped through the chart as he walked, and went to cause of death—MYOCARDIAL INFARCTION. The case seemed straightforward enough, a heart attack out in the field, CPR all the way in during the ambulance ride, full cardiac arrest team in the ER working on him for over half an hour. What was so different about this? Ralph checked the attending physician on duty that night. Dr. Samantha Nolan. When he looked up, he found himself standing in front of his desk. He locked up the office until he could hear the deadbolt on his door snap shut twice. He shook the lock to make sure it was tight.

On his way through the parking lot, he asked himself why he had to park so far away from the staff entrance. He'd been at this hospital for decades; you'd think they'd humor him with a closer parking pass. His keys jiggled in the silence followed by the click of the car door opener releasing the security system.

Ralph opened the driver's side door, but before he could get in, he felt a club hit him in the back of his head like a thunderbolt, and the light from the lamppost faded into darkness.

THE ICU

The EKG monitor of the ICU room kept a regular musical rhythm. Ralph's ventilator tried to keep pace, but the in and out sucking noise had a pace of its own. It had been three days and Ralph's grey beard was starting to show. Nurse Peggy wasn't about to add a beeping IV line to the orchestra of sounds. She pressed every button she could on the IV pole just to get some semblance of peace and quiet.

"Good to have you back, Dr. Nolan."

Sam hadn't left Ralph's side since she hopped the redeye thirty-six hours ago to be with him. She also hadn't gotten any sleep during that time. Ralph, whom she'd always looked to for vision and guidance, couldn't even open his eyes now. She didn't notice Pete in the doorway. Sam didn't take her eyes off Ralph when she spoke.

"I'm just visiting Dr. Peyton, Peggy. I'm going back to my sabbatical tomorrow."

"Sorry to hear that, Dr. Nolan. We really miss you when

you're not here." Peggy slammed the IV device shut, hoping she could beat the beeping sound out of it.

"Yes, I'm sorry to hear that, too." Pete's leather-bottomed loafers screeched against the freshly waxed floor.

Sam recognized his voice and saw Pete standing at the foot of Ralph's bed. His gold detective's shield hung around his neck, framed by the worn tan coat. She had tried for years to get him to buy a new overcoat, but he said it was too much a part of his life for him to part with it. He always did have trouble letting go.

"Pete, this is horrible. I feel like it's my fault."

"They think it was an attempted carjacking gone bad," he said.

He sat down in the plastic chair next to her. It was hard and not very comfortable, but he didn't care. Pete noticed her skin more tanned than usual for this time of year. She must be outside a lot up there. With twenty-three hours of the midnight sun, he wasn't surprised. Sam shook her head from side to side, fighting back tears.

"I don't believe it. This whole thing is out of control."

"You could always come back," Pete leaned into Sam, "permanently." It was the same perfume, the one that reminded him of the trip they had taken to the beach.

"I feel I owe you a firm decision, Pete." Sam pulled her knit sweater across her chest. Suddenly she felt cold.

"I'm going back to Woodbridge," she said, motionless.

"For good?" Pete cleared his throat.

Sam finally looked up at him. She had changed her lipstick to a softer color, and her cheeks were smooth, with a new kind of glow. Her dark eyes were still the same kind you could get lost in, only deeper now.

"For now." She hesitated. "But I want to go back."

Pete got up and started making his way to the glass door. The room didn't seem very bright, even with the lights on. He loosened his black and blue striped tie and threw his sports jacket over his shoulder. He stood just outside the doorway and faced Sam.

"I understand. I don't like it, Sam, but I understand." Pete took off his badge and tucked it in his pants pocket.

"Good-bye, and be careful."

"I will," she said and waved.

Nurse Peggy suctioned out thick green sputum from Ralph's tracheal tube. "I know it's private but may I ask where you've been?"

"Woodbridge, Alaska. I'm helping out a friend of Dr. Peyton's." Sam figured it was okay. Working in healthcare, Peggy understood confidentiality.

Sam stood next to Ralph and held his hand in hers. The sweat began to drip off the sides of Ralph's forehead onto his pillow. He looked so rested for someone who was fighting for his life. Sam ran a washcloth under cold tap water. She squeezed the terry fabric until it felt like an ice cube in her hands, then patted every inch of Ralph's face.

"I'd go crazy in a place like that," Nurse Peggy remarked. "What do you possibly do up there?"

"I enjoy…the wildlife." Sam smiled.

THE NURSE'S STATION

Nurse Peggy rummaged through the front station to scrounge up another bag of fluids for Ralph's IV. *You'd think with all the money this hospital was putting into showing off to the community, they'd make sure we had enough supplies to take care of the patients.* Since Ralph wouldn't be eating for a few days, he needed as much sustenance as possible. She combed through all the bags, until she found exactly the right mixture. As soon as this crisis passed and Dr. Peyton was well, he'd be off and running again. She wanted to make sure his nutrition was able to keep up with him.

Wanda Cunningham had started as ward clerk three years ago, but in that short period of time she had made life easier for everyone. The counters were finally clean, no messy papers or pens strewn about. The filing cabinets had real files in them, orderly and labeled so the nurses could find all their documents in a hurry. No sifting through every piece of paper. Orders got taken off and put into the computer on time. It was a medical professional's dream.

Wanda's father was an old Navy man from way back. The first and only black man in his unit. He grew up poor and overworked, and wanted to make sure Wanda got a better life. She did.

"Was that our Dr. Sam I saw floating around, Peggy? She just flew in and out. Where's she been? I miss her," Wanda said as she filed all the scattered patient charts neatly into the medical records carousel.

"She's out on a sabbatical for a while," Nurse Peggy answered.

Nurse Peggy kept her eyes on the medication roster. She knew one mistake could cost her job. Wanda took a stack of lab results and started putting them in alphabetical order. She was glad to wear her rubber-tipped cover over her second finger. It made her thumb through the papers a lot faster. She grabbed a pen from her desk drawer and stuck it in her scrub pocket. A ward clerk can never have enough pens. They sprout legs and walk, especially when more people are on duty.

Nurse Peggy put the medication log in front of Wanda to sign. A medical records courier walked up to the station and leaned against the counter as if to take a rest, waiting to get Wanda's attention.

"This place is definitely a lot less colorful without Dr. Sam. I bet Kurt in Radiology she'd punch out Clyde before the year's end. Is she coming back soon?" Wanda asked. She had a $100 on the bet and planned to collect.

"I don't know. She's heading back to a Woodbridge, Alaska, to finish some work up there."

Nurse Peggy didn't look up as she rechecked the medication log sheet one more time. Wanda extended her hand to the courier and pointed to the basket.

"Thank you, just leave the file there."

Wanda went back to her desk and the laundry list of orders she needed to enter into the computer before shift's end. Nurse Peggy scurried back to Dr. Peyton's room. It was time to recheck his ventilator settings.

The medical records courier picked up her pace and headed toward the elevator.

THE CLINIC

They were lucky it was a sunny day. Their job would've been a lot harder and messier to accomplish in the rain. Jack and Ron held the sign, while Ray fixed it firmly into the ground. Patients wouldn't miss it as they walked into the clinic. Ron had spent two weeks and too many late nights in his wood-shop getting it ready. His wife said she'd never be able to get the smoldering smell of burnt wood out of Ron's clothes. It was worth it when she saw how beautifully etched the words sunk into the background.

Millie came outside to give the final approval for the project. She loved wearing her jeans and denim shirt to the clinic. It was the only time she felt comfortable. She could get away with it today, a Sunday afternoon.

Jamie saw the gathering of the crowd outside the clinic from the café window. She put down her steaming pot of coffee to go outside and take a break, mostly to get away from the stale smell of greasy hamburgers and fries. Anytime more than three people in Woodbridge got together, something was going on. Diving into everyone else's business was the only way to break the monotony.

"Hey, Dr. Sam," Millie called and waved.

Sam pulled up in her car with the window down. She realized how much she liked fresh air, especially in Woodbridge. She was still wearing her city clothes, a beige skirt, Ralph Lauren navy sweater, and dark pumps from her recent trip. She couldn't wait to get out of the car, kick off her shoes and find out what all the fuss was about.

Ron found this a lot easier to settle in than the 214-piece dollhouse he'd put together for his daughter last Christmas.

"What's this?" Sam asked.

"Lift it up on that side, Jack, so I can secure it," Ron said in a strained voice.

"Is this okay?" Jack let go.

"Don't hurt yourself, my work injury rates are through the roof already," Ray joked.

"We didn't expect you till tomorrow, Dr. Sam. We wanted to surprise you when it was already in." Millie noticed Skye in the distance walking toward Sam.

"Hey Skye, d'ya see what we got here for Doc?" Jamie shouted out.

She waved Skye over toward Sam. Sam pulled up her sweater sleeves and tried to fix her hair at lightning speed. Skye crouched down to get a good look at the sign. His unbuttoned shirt fell open at the sides and showed his white T-shirt hugging the front of his chest before settling into his rough and worn jeans. They outlined every curve of his leg muscles.

"Look at that—guess you have your own clinic now, Doc," Millie said.

"Looks like it," Sam answered with a grin.

Millie pulled Sam away from the crowd while everyone else gawked at the new sign. It was just an excuse for everyone to hang out before either getting back to football or Sunday dinner with in-laws, the latter resulting frequently in Monday morning requests for sedatives from Sam.

"I hope you're not angry, Dr. Sam." Millie frowned. "I had them make it so your name could come off pretty easy."

"Millie, it's just fine the way it is."

Sam looked past Millie to Skye. He noticed her glance and headed over. Sam admired his distinctive, athletic gait and didn't take her eyes off him. She soaked in every moment of Skye that she could. Skye looked Sam up and down, then cracked a smile himself. He stepped closer to her, and she couldn't tell if the heavy musk scent was the woods or his cologne. It didn't matter; she took in a deep breath and held on to it as long as she could.

"Everything okay at home?"

"Ralph's hurt, but he's gonna make it."

"Everyone else okay?" Skye stuck his hands in his pockets, then bit the side of his lip.

"I saw Pete briefly, very briefly. I told him I was coming back here because I still had more work to do."

"Is that so?"

Sam pulled the barrette out of her hair and let her chestnut locks fall to her shoulders. Skye took his hands out of his pockets and brushed a stray hair off Sam's face and to the side. Millie caught a glimpse of them talking and nudged Ray's arm. It stayed sunny for the rest of the afternoon.

THE ICU

Nurse Lahia couldn't get enough of the 8 a.m. to 8 p.m. shift. She was older now, her children grown and she could make two to three dollars more per hour than the day shifters. She lived to save her money for relaxing trips back to Hawaii to see her relatives. She was the only one of her siblings to move to the mainland. That's what happens when you marry a government employee. Your life becomes theirs.

Lahia knew Ralph wasn't tired, but it still was two hours until his scheduled sleeping pill. Ralph cleared his throat. His lips were parched from all of his mouth breathing. He didn't care, he was just glad to get rid of his tracheal tube.

"Dr. Peyton, there's a Detective Garren Taylor outside to see you. Feel up to seeing him?"

"I'm okay, I can see him, Lahia." Ralph straightened up and pressed the button to raise the head of his electronic bed. He caught a glimpse of himself in the mirror and noticed how gray his beard had become. He was glad he stayed clean-shaven at the hospital. He didn't want the interns to know how much of an old man he really was.

"Detective Taylor, Dr. Peyton will see you now. Just keep it short, he's still weak."

"Yes, ma'am." Taylor nodded.

Nurse Lahia stepped out into the hallway. She stood close to the doorway so she could keep an eye on Ralph. She didn't want Taylor to say or do anything that would upset him. She kept the blood pressure and pulse monitor within her sights. A patient's status could change in a heartbeat, literally. It was a good rule to live by. Ralph gave her the eye for an upcoming confidential conversation.

"Hello, Detective Taylor. Fine mess I got myself into." Ralph coughed.

Taylor tried to hand him one of those hospital tissues that feels coarse enough to exfoliate your face, but Ralph shook his head no. He took a seat next to Ralph's bed. Ralph pushed his control switch to raise his bed to Taylor's level. Even sitting down, Taylor was a giant. Taylor pulled a small, wire-bound notepad out of his coat pocket and flipped through the pages. He stopped when he found the section he wanted. He took his Cross pen from his shirt pocket and clicked it on, ready to record Ralph.

"Your secretary called me and she said you told her you were well enough to meet with me."

"Check the table over there for that file."

Ralph waved Taylor's notepad down. He pointed to a manila file on the wood-grained aluminum table on the other side of the room. Taylor put his memo pad and pen on the stand next to Ralph's steel-framed bed. He walked toward the table and as he grew closer, he could read in bold, black letters, "Patient Medical Record" on the front with an ID# scrolled on a white label. He checked the index tab on the side, "Dwyer, Lawrence." Taylor shook his head up and down in both surprise and relief. He tried to patch the worn, tattered end of the file back into place. This was a precious piece of evidence. Taylor sat back in his chair and scratched his chin as he thumbed through the file.

Taylor's Bruno Magli shoes seemed comfortable attached to his confident frame. No one was less impressed by them than Taylor. They served a purpose. He couldn't be accused of being just another grunt gumshoe. He stopped and looked up at Ralph.

"You found him; this is a big break."

"I don't know. Dr. Nolan was the emergency room physician who treated him when he came in, but he was in the ER for less than an hour."

"How so?" Taylor asked.

"Looks like he had a massive heart attack before he even hit the front door. There was very little Sam could do by that point."

"Doesn't a medical record always have a next of kin?"

"The demographic page lists the closest relatives. Check the very front of the chart." Ralph started a coughing fit that couldn't stop.

Taylor put down the file and grabbed the plastic pitcher of ice water. The beads of condensation were still dripping down the outside of the container. The water felt cool and would go down cold into Ralph's throat. He poured a glass of water for Ralph and stuck a straw in it. He bent the flexible neck and fed it to Ralph, who finished it off before Taylor could get back to the chart. Ralph was ready for more interviewing. This was Sam's life they were talking about. Taylor scanned the demographic page and pointed to the bottom. Ralph took a deep breath and struggled to sit up higher. He winced in pain.

"Here it is. Only one person is listed, a Lorraine Kester, 119 Mason Street." Taylor thumbed through the rest of file, not sure what he might be looking for.

"Detective Taylor, I took a Hippocratic Oath to be kind and care for people."

"Yes, sir."

"But not this time. Catch this guy, and throw away the key."

Taylor closed the file and gripped it in his hand like a fist. Ralph pressed the bedside power button and sat himself up as high as he could. Taylor leaned back in his chair, still clutching the file. The room grew quiet. They listened to the steady beat of Ralph's heart on the monitor. It sounded a lot stronger now.

LORRAINE KESTER

This was never the best part of town. Taylor had worked this beat when he first got out of the academy, and he had hoped he would never have to return here again. The streets had the smoldering smell of raw sewage that rose up onto the sidewalks, especially on 90-degree days. The kids from juvie were cleaning up the graffiti they got busted for, only to leave it an open canvas for the next gang. Everybody did their turn around here.

The green and white street sign was half shot off to show only "MAS." The blue paint on the side of the house looked like it had been cracking for years, not months. Next to the weathered front door was the muddied number 19. Taylor opened the gate of the aluminum chain link fence, old and noisy with squeaks. By the time he took two steps, the gate shut and locked itself. He figured the doorbell probably didn't work, so he knocked instead.

A gray-haired woman in her late sixties wearing a heather brown sweater answered the door. She pulled her sweater inward to cover herself from the cool breeze that rushed in the doorway.

"Lorraine Kester?" Taylor asked.

Lorraine pulled the top of the two sides of her sweater together, revealing a small hole in the knitting that showed the fabric of her blouse below. The knuckles of both her hands were swollen on her disjointed fingers. She winced a little when she tightened her grip. Lorraine brushed her gray hair off the side of her face so she could take a closer look at Taylor. Taylor flashed his badge.

"I'm Detective Garren Taylor. I need to ask you some questions about Larry Dwyer."

"Larry died over two years ago. How can I help you?"

"Yes, ma'am, I know, but his name turned up in an investigation and I only need some routine information."

Lorraine pushed open the screen door. Taylor grabbed the edge and pulled it all the way because he could tell she couldn't keep it open on her own. He took a step into the foyer and breathed in the musty, grandma-like smell of a house that hadn't had a spring cleaning in several years. The colors of the furniture, deep rose, washed-out forest green, and dirty beige lay hidden beneath a layer of collective dust. Her green and black striped cat meowed from behind a scratched antique table. It peered at Taylor. Visitors were rare in this household.

146

"Come right in, sir," she waved him forward, "I was just taking my afternoon tea."

He stepped forward toward a wing chair with intricately carved legs. It was the only highlight of the room.

Lorraine sat in the deep-cushioned chair nearest the kitchen. Taylor settled into the wing chair. He cleared his throat and took a deep breath. He had grown used to the smell of the room by now. Taylor pulled his pad from his overcoat pocket. He flipped through the tattered pages making a rustling sound that caught the cat's attention. He clicked open his pen and flattened out the blank page with his hand.

"Tea, Detective?" Lorraine raised her eyebrows. She picked up the antique ivory teapot with dark pink roses surrounded by gold leaf etched into the sides and started pouring for herself. Its elegance stood out in stark contrast to the rest of the room.

"No thank you, ma'am."

"I thought Larry died from a heart attack. Why would anyone be investigating his death now?"

"You were listed as Larry's spouse; were you married long?"

"Just under six years, but they were all wonderful. Larry was a kind and gentle man." She nodded softly with a smile. The steam from the teacup moistened her upper lip as she took a sip.

"If I may ask, ma'am, why do you have a different last name from Larry?" Taylor started scribbling some notes.

"It was a second marriage for both of us. I had Kester so long, I didn't want the inconvenience of a name change. My first husband died of lung cancer."

"And Mr. Dwyer's first wife, what happened to her?"

The room grew cold. Lorraine hesitated, then took another sip of tea. Her hands shook and she tried to set the teacup back onto the center of the saucer, but it scraped the china and knocked the spoon onto the floor. Taylor picked it up for her and she set it aside on a napkin.

"Ms. Kester?"

Taylor dropped his eyes toward Lorraine's sunken look. She waited, then raised her expression to his.

"Larry didn't like to talk about it much. His first wife, Susan K. Dwyer, had a severe drinking problem."

"Go on."

Taylor sat back in his chair. The stiff back of the wing chair supported him and he felt more comfortable, especially about where their conversation was going.

"Susan K., or Kim, as she liked to be called, would go into fits of angry rages and beat Larry, right in front of their child. Eventually, she lost all contact with the real world, and he had her committed to the state hospital. She died ten years ago."

"And their son?" Taylor scribbled rapid notes on his pad.

"Son? They never had a son," Lorraine replied.

Taylor stopped writing. He furrowed his eyebrows together. "You said their child."

"I meant their daughter. They only had one child, a daughter, Janelle Dwyer."

Lorraine picked up a framed photo off the fireplace mantle and handed it to Taylor. Larry looked tall, but the petite blonde he cradled around his arm didn't look like she stood more than five feet. He handed it back to Lorraine.

"Where might I find Janelle?"

"She's Janelle Roamer now, married, then divorced." She wiped the dust off the top of the frame and placed the photo gently back into its spot on the mantle.

"I always felt she got more of her mother than Larry."

Lorraine stepped into the dining room and pulled down the front of the desk secretary. She anchored the wooden plank and brought it down while the side metal plackets squeaked themselves into position.

Taylor got up and started looking at the wall of family photos carefully displayed in the dining room. He recognized Larry with three other guys, all wearing Pacific Western Insurance T-shirts.

"Since Larry died, Janelle doesn't keep up with me much." Lorraine wrote on a slip of paper and handed it to Taylor. "This is her last known address."

Taylor pointed to the photo of Larry and his buddies. "Pacific Western Insurance?"

"Larry worked there for thirty years before he died." She pursed her lips.

Taylor focused on a photo of Janelle in hospital scrubs and a white lab coat, standing next to Lorraine. He touched the edge of the photo frame.

"When was this photo taken?"

"It was a couple months ago. Janelle said since Larry died at Memorial Hospital, she wanted to get a job there and help out any way she could."

Lorraine walked Taylor to the front door and opened the screen.

"I'm sorry, Detective, I couldn't be of more help to you. It's still difficult for me to talk about Larry's death."

Lorraine stepped outside with Taylor. He headed toward the front steps and turned around when he was halfway down.

"You've been more than helpful. Thank you, ma'am. I'll be in touch if I have any more questions."

MIRANDA

This must have been the tenth time this week Miranda found herself vacuuming the living room carpet. Her German shepherd, Rainbow, had decided it was finally time to shed her winter coat. Miranda felt the contractions and they seemed more intense. She thought a basketball was falling down into her pelvis, and it was. She dropped to the floor into a puddle of water. The contractions were now only minutes apart. She could barely crawl to the phone and dial the clinic's number.

"Woodbridge Clinic, Millie speaking. May I help you?" The voice wasn't recognizable with the rhythmic noise of the vacuum cleaner in the background.

"Miranda, is that you? I can't hear you, the vacuum cleaner's on. What, you spilled the water...no, your water broke! I'll get Dr. Sam."

"Dr. Nolan, I need you right away," Millie screeched from the reception desk. Sam barged out of the exam room, gloves on with her stethoscope swaying around her neck.

"Millie, are you okay?"

"I'm fine, but it's Miranda. Her water broke. She's alone and can't get down the mountain."

"I was afraid this was going to happen." Sam took off her gloves and threw them in the garbage. She shut the exam room door and pulled her stethoscope off her neck.

"What am I supposed to do? She can't get here?" Sam remembered from her intern days how babies have a habit of always coming at the most inconvenient times.

"I'll call Skye on the walkie-talkie. Meet him at the base camp. He'll get you up there." Millie searched through all the wooden desk drawers until the walkie-talkie fell out of the last one she opened. Sam grabbed her jacket halfway out the door and yelled back to Millie.

"Reschedule Mrs. Lambert to the end of the week. Tell Skye to have the truck ready. We don't have much time."

Sam pulled her car up as far as she could get to the base camp. It was the middle of the day and the carrying crane was in full gear, drowning out every sound, all the way into town. The wood chips created a thick blanket of shavings over the ground, with an occasional log piercing through and pushing up against the soles of Sam's boots. The fresh pine branches had fallen from cutting, softening the smell of oil and grease. They rubbed against Sam's leg like a heavy feather as she rushed to find Skye.

"Jack, lower that choke hold, or you'll be eating bark for dinner." Skye waved the crane in.

"I'm on it, Skye." Jack pointed to Sam coming toward Skye.

151

She cupped her hands around her mouth as she shouted, "Skye, I need to get up the—"

Skye dropped his work belt and started heading toward Sam, saying, "I know Sam, Millie called me and we don't have much time, get in."

Skye started up the truck while Sam raced to grab her doctor's bag from the back seat of her car. She had thought it was ridiculous at the time to buy a doctor's bag. Especially an overpriced rose-fabric designer bag from Nordstrom's. Little did she know that the moment would come when she was glad she had stuck to her inner dorky self. Skye buckled up and made sure Sam did too. He knew how rugged these rides could get, and they didn't need any more casualties on the mountain. Besides, Sam was with him and she had grown too important to take any unnecessary risks, but she didn't know that. He wanted to keep it that way. Skye pressed hard on the walkie-talkie and drove with the other hand.

"Millie, Sam's here and I'm taking her up. We'll call you from the land line when we get up there."

Skye put the walkie-talkie down between himself and Sam. She pushed it out of the way and folded his hand into hers. Skye tightened his grip and held on to Sam as he stepped on the gas up the mountain.

JANELLE ROAMER

The blonde at the reception desk stood still and unassuming while Millie had her back to her and faced the shelf of charts set out for the next day. The visitor focused on the plaque on the countertop, Samantha Nolan, M.D.

Millie's voice registered a welcome calm into the walkie-talkie. "Thanks, Skye, you guys call me right away when you get up there. I'll send Ray to base camp."

Millie poured herself a glass of ice water and gulped most of it down. She dipped a paper towel into what was left and wiped her brow and face with the cool relief. She turned to see her visitor scanning Sam's diplomas on the side wall.

"Yes, ma'am, how may I help you?" Millie didn't recognize her from around the area.

"I'm Janelle Roamer and Dr. Ralph Peyton sent me. He said Dr. Nolan was going to be staying up here for a while and she would need a medical assistant."

Millie noticed her jacket bottom had a ripped edge and broken zipper. She had her hair down, stringy at the ends. Usually, hospital personnel have their hair up most of the time. Her coat smelled of a freshly smoked cigarette. Millie recognized that from thirty years with loggers.

"Really?" Millie hesitated. "Dr. Peyton hasn't called here to tell us he was sending someone."

The woman pulled out a half-folded envelope from her worn plastic handbag. The strap was broken on one side and small threads fell off the bottom. She took out of the envelope a letter with hospital letterhead and Dr. Peyton's signature on it and handed it over to Millie.

"Oh, I know Dr. Peyton wanted me to be discrete. His secretary gave me this letter and asked that I include my resume and hospital credential when I presented it to you." She spoke quickly with a direct smile.

Millie brought her eyes down to use her bifocals. The letter felt like regular business parchment, along with the resume and copy of her hospital photo ID. Her smile in the photo lacked enthusiasm and warmth, almost forced.

"It looks like everything is in order. Let's get started then. I'll show you around."

Millie unlocked the gate in the hallway and led Janelle to the back of the clinic. Janelle peered around the corner and down the path to the exam rooms.

"Where's Dr. Nolan now?"

"She had an emergency up the mountain. She's up there delivering a baby with Skye." Janelle stopped walking and looked at Millie.

"Skye?" Her face tightened around her mouth and her left cheek muscle started to twitch. Millie shut Sam's office door, which had been left open in Sam's rush to leave.

"Skye Ronan. He's hooktender, foreman as they say, at our logging camp. He's Dr. Nolan's company…friend." Millie left it at that.

Janelle broke into a wide-eyed smile. She dropped her shoulders and unzipped her jacket. "I understand." That she did.

MIRANDA

The room was hot, even with all the windows open. Sam put the portable fan on full force to lace Miranda with some semblance of a breeze. Skye couldn't put cold towels fast enough on her forehead. Steam rose from Miranda's burning face and temples. The contractions were coming even closer together as were Miranda's screams.

"God, somebody get this baby out!" Miranda noticed the crack in the ceiling that her Adam had never gotten around to fixing before he died. It didn't seem to matter much today. Miranda reached out and Skye took her left hand. She was wearing her wedding ring. Skye remembered the day he and Adam had picked out Miranda's engagement ring. It was still shining as brightly as the day she got it, even more so.

"I'm right here, Miranda, and the head's down," Sam yelled from the end of the bed.

"Get it out!" Miranda let out several short, quick puffs of air. Sam kept turning her hands from side to side.

"Skye, you gotta help me. I can't get the umbilical cord down. It's my injury, I can't use my thumb."

Skye's face dropped and he tightened his grip on Miranda. "What the hell do you want me to do?"

"You're gonna have to deliver the baby. I'll walk you through it."

"I can't, Sam."

Miranda screamed again, and let go of Skye's hand. She

grabbed Skye by the arm and pushed him toward her feet. "Get down there right now, Skye, and help her!"

"You've got to. Now look at me, Skye," Sam insisted.

Skye focused his gaze directly into Sam's eyes. Not a very difficult thing for him to do. He scrambled to put on some exam gloves. It felt like he was tugging on them for hours in order for them to fit right.

"You can do this. We can do this." Sam spoke with concentration.

"Okay, okay." Skye blew out a long, deep breath. He was sweating more than Miranda by now.

"Bring the umbilical cord over the head."

"Like this?" Skye's hands were trembling.

"Exactly, not too fast, not too hard, easy." Sam nodded her approval.

"It's coming slowly." Skye's hands felt like ice, even through the gloves. Sam rubbed the outside of Miranda's thigh in comfort.

"Miranda, when I tell you to, you're gonna push real hard and Skye's gonna catch the baby."

"Great," Skye mumbled under his breath.

"Ready, Miranda?" Sam's voice accelerated.

"Let's go, I've been ready for hours," Miranda yelled.

"One...Skye, pull down," Sam signaled.

"I'm pulling," Skye winced.

"Two...okay Miranda, push hard...three!"

"Oh my God, all this blood." Skye saw his hands and arms drenched in red liquid.

"Skye, not so vocal," Sam whispered in his ear.

There was a long pause that made everything stand still, even the air, and then a loud, healthy cry.

"It's a girl!" Sam's eyes widened to match the smile on Miranda's face.

"Look at all that hair," Skye said, laughing.

Sam had Skye hold the baby while she cut the umbilical cord. He wiped the blood and mucous away from the baby's skin. He cradled her in the yellow and green blanket Miranda had saved for this special occasion. He wouldn't give her to Sam; he kept holding her and rocking her back and forth.

"She looks so peaceful." Skye held her close to his chest.

Sam placed her hand behind Skye's neck. "I totally understand."

Skye leaned forward toward Sam, when Miranda lifted her head up. "Excuse me, who did the work? Can I see her now?"

Skye brought the baby to Miranda and laid her gently across Miranda's chest. Miranda's joy was mixed with tears that her Adam couldn't be here on this day. They always knew logging was a dangerous job and the forest is unforgiving, but having her new baby made Miranda feel that a part of her Adam would stay alive.

"And a name?" Sam stroked the baby's soft face.

"Mirelle," Miranda replied in a flash.

"What does Mirelle mean?" Skye was intrigued. He sat down in the chair next to Miranda's bed. He felt as if he had just logged the entire mountain by himself.

"It's French, for miracle." Miranda put her right index finger in Mirelle's hand. Her little angel hung on tight.

"There have been a lot of miracles lately," Sam winked at Skye.

"You both look beat. I need to head back to the clinic. Miranda, you gonna be okay?"

Skye stared at Mirelle, then looked at Sam. "I'll stay for a little while, then meet you in town. Take the truck, I'll walk back down."

Miranda wiped the last elements of sweat from her brow.

"You go, Dr. Sam. I'll be fine now."

Sam started to slip on her jacket and head toward the front door. She turned to see Skye right behind her.

"I'll grab us some food and meet you at your cabin for lunch, or do you have to get back to base camp right away?"

Skye stood in the front of the hallway, larger than life to Sam now. She could feel herself sinking deeper into Skye's aura. Delivering Mirelle together gave her another layer of connection that made her closer to Skye, no matter how hard she tried to keep distance between them. It just wasn't going to happen anymore.

"If you're buyin' lunch, you think I'm gonna pass that up?"

Sam picked up Miranda's phone on the front table next to the door and dialed out.

"Millie, we're done. Mirelle Lakeland and mother Miranda are both doing fine."

JANELLE

Janelle sat patiently in the waiting room, listening to Millie on the phone. She pretended to peruse the year-old *Good House-keeping* magazine while she watched Millie. The warm scent of the freshly brewed afternoon coffee drifted over to her from the hospitality table.

"That's great, Sam. You heading right back?" Millie lifted her index finger to Janelle, to let her know it would be just a minute. Janelle motioned to Millie toward the back of the clinic, then mouthed the word bathroom.

Millie covered the receiver. "Down the hall."

Janelle exited into the hallway, then snuck into the lab. She picked up the phone extension and recognized the voice on the other end. She stood behind the door to the lab and kept the light off. A sudden loud click startled Janelle. She covered her mouth so Millie and Sam couldn't hear her on the line. She felt a hot whisk of steam at the back of her neck from the autoclave that had just shut off. Millie didn't budge from her seat. It was a regular sound in the clinic, nothing out of the ordinary to her.

"I'm stopping at the café and picking up some food." Sam took the barrette out of her hair. It was getting heavy and she was getting a headache. She figured she was probably a little dehydrated, too, from all the action. "I'll be meeting Skye at his cabin for lunch."

"Isn't it kind of early in the day, Dr. Sam?" Millie questioned in her low voice.

"You're a filthy-minded woman, Millie."

Janelle pressed her thumb against the telephone base and edged the receiver back onto the line.

"Why do you think I've been married so long? See you when you get here," Millie said with a laugh.

Janelle fluffed her blonde hair and licked her lips, as if she had just freshened up in the bathroom. She entered the waiting room and shut the hallway door behind her. Janelle stepped up to Millie and placed her hands on the counter. Millie didn't take Janelle for a nervous girl, yet her fingernails were nearly chewed to the bone.

"Everything okay?" Janelle forced a smile.

"That was just Dr. Nolan. She's heading back to the clinic, but she's stopping at the café for some lunch."

"Oh, I can wait for her." Janelle took off her jacket and hung it on the antique coat rack near the front door. She sat in the chair next to the Office Depot side table. She pulled an apple out of her handbag and started chomping away. This time she picked up a People magazine.

Millie scrambled for a way to get Janelle out of there before she could settle in.

"She should be back around two o'clock for her afternoon patients."

"No problem. I'll go check into the motel and be back later." Janelle didn't want to push it too much.

"Thank you, Janelle. I'm sure Dr. Sam will be glad to have you here." Millie noticed the hole in the back of Janelle's jeans as she headed toward the door. Not the kind you find intentionally in designer jeans.

Janelle turned and grabbed her jacket from the coat rack.

"I hope so. I've been waiting for months to see her again."

The warm wind streamed across Janelle's face. It was just what she wanted. She opened the gasoline cans and the fumes initially overpowered the scent of pine trees and dried bark around her. She felt several branches break under her hiking boots as she spread the liquid all along the brush on the side of the road. The matchstick crackled against the flint. A blue and orange flame shot up. It quickly captured the surrounding bushes and spread like a sea of uncontrolled chimney fires in every direction. She walked back toward town, taking her time.

THE ROOSTER CAFÉ

Janelle sat in her car in the last parking spot outside The Rooster Café. She crouched down when she saw Sam pull up in Skye's pickup truck, then scurry into the café. Jamie strolled with the coffee pot and filled up all the guests at the counter. She pulled another mug off the shelf when she saw Sam walk in. Doctors love coffee: morning, noon, night, and every time in between.

"Hey, Dr. Sam, an early lunch for you?" Jamie poured. She could do it blindfolded and in her sleep after so many years.

Sam unzipped her jacket, and let out a sigh from her reddened, windblown face.

"I just got down from the mountain. Miranda had the baby, a girl."

Jamie clanked down the coffee pot and raised her arms in relief. "Hallelujah, now I can buy the pink booties instead of Sponge Bob."

"Sponge Bob?" Sam didn't even finish half her coffee. "I'll take two bacon cheeseburger meals to go." So what if she was a doctor. She was entitled to her fair share of unadulterated fat and comfort food like the rest of America.

Jamie wrote down the order and laughed. She felt vindicated to see her doctor willingly eat that much cholesterol.

Janelle rushed into the café catching her breath. The bell over the doorway struck the glass door, which shut tight behind her.

"Dr. Nolan," Janelle puffed.

"Yes, I'm Dr. Nolan."

"I'm Janelle. Millie asked me to come down right away and find you." Janelle brushed her hair out of her eyes and away from her face. She sat with her back to Jamie and spoke in a low voice. She wanted to keep the conversation just between her and Sam.

"Is there a problem at the clinic?" Sam sat on the counter stool and finished off the rest of the coffee.

"A man came to the clinic looking for you. Millie didn't feel right about it, so she's stalling him. She asked me to come down here and find you. She said don't come back to the clinic just yet, and I should go with you to Skye's cabin until Skye gets back there."

Sam stepped off the counter stool and stood in front of Janelle. She didn't recognize Janelle from anywhere in town or at the clinic.

"Who is this man?"

"He said his name was Larry and his father knew your father."

Janelle kept her eyes fixed on Sam, waiting for a response. Sam pulled out her worn leather wallet and headed toward the cash register.

"Jamie, I gotta go. Can I get those meals?"

Jamie rushed the food to Sam, still steaming. "Here you go, Doc. Don't worry, I'll charge the clinic."

Sam lead Janelle out the door and into Skye's truck. She pulled out of the parking lot, gunning the engine and scraping the gravel as they headed toward the cabin. Jamie watched from the side window as they disappeared out of sight. She picked up the phone and dialed Millie.

"That's okay, Jamie, she knows Dr. Sam from her hospital. The hospital sent her up here to work. Thanks for calling."

Millie turned off the lights and headed out the back door. Jamie hung up the receiver and watched Millie pull her car out of the driveway. The clinic had never looked so quiet and empty to her.

THE FIRE

Gladys peered out her kitchen window to catch a glimpse of the rising gray smoke threatening the Wynack house less than half a mile away. Fire was feared on the mountain, more than a windstorm or all the trees that could possibly fall down. It was the ultimate enemy to anything in its path.

"Nine-one-one; what are you reporting?" the dispatcher droned.

"There's smoke, and I think there's a fire heading north on Colby Lane."

Gladys ran out to her car, coughing from breathing in the rising embers along the way. She took off into town, hoping to find as many people as she could.

GARREN TAYLOR AND RALPH PEYTON

Taylor drew diagram after diagram on his notepad. None of the pieces of the puzzle made any sense to him; in fact, the whole puzzle didn't make any sense to him anymore. He fidgeted with his tie. He wanted to look good in the doctor's office, even if he wasn't a patient.

Ralph Peyton shut the door behind him and sat at his desk.

The rolled up sleeves of his white coat and morning shadow gave away a hard night in the ER.

"Sorry to keep you waiting, Detective. I got trapped in the ER."

"No problem, I'm a cop. I don't like ERs." Taylor put his hand on his hip and leaned back in his chair.

"Find anything?" Ralph rubbed his eyes while yawning. A trick he had learned in residency to help him wake up faster. It didn't work anymore. A sure sign he was getting older.

"Larry Dwyer never had a son." Taylor closed his notes.

Ralph opened his eyes and sat up.

"He had a daughter, Janelle Dwyer, now Janelle Roamer." Taylor handed Ralph a photo. "Stepmother gave me her address. I followed her a few days ago and took this photo."

"I know this girl." Ralph scratched the back of his scalp searching for the connection. He flicked the photo in his hand, straining for a connection.

"Stepmom thinks she may have gotten a job here."

Ralph swiveled in his chair to face his computer. He typed in several different entries until he heard the tone of the one beep he wanted to hear and Janelle's photo popped up on the screen.

"Detective, you'll want to see this."

Taylor pulled his chair around to sit next to Ralph. They both scanned the screen until Janelle's personnel file appeared. Ralph pointed to the demographic sheet.

"That's her: Janelle Roamer, maiden name Dwyer, medical records assistant, date of hire—"

"Do you still have Larry Dwyer's chart?" Taylor jumped in.

Ralph pulled the chart out from the bottom of a stack on a

side desk. Taylor flipped through the back section referring to Dwyer's ER admission.

"What?" Ralph watched Taylor's gaze scramble from the back of the chart to the front of his notes.

"Look at her date of hire. Janelle Roamer was hired after Larry Dwyer's death and before Dr. Nolan started getting the death threats."

Ralph got back to the computer screen and typed in several codes.

"Oh no!" Ralph sighed, dropping his shoulders.

"What is it?" Taylor wasn't sure he even wanted to know the answer to his own question.

"There's an entry here in her file that Roamer is taking a personal leave of absence for ten days, starting two days ago," Ralph said quickly.

Taylor loosened his tie and slumped back in his chair and tapped his finger on his leg.

"You can sure bet its personal," Taylor said, nodding.

MEDICAL RECORDS

Karen knew that a sense of humor was useful, no, an absolute necessity for her position as medical records director. She riffled through the multicolored files, of which only a half dozen or so employees could follow her elaborate system. Jennifer, one of the rare and the few who could sort them out, pulled a large wire cart toward the basket marked "Incoming." The mismatched files made a haiku of colors that left a stark contrast against the background of cold, gray, steel shelves. Karen started sorting through the new arrivals.

Jennifer lined up the different page tags: hot pink, bright blue, electric orange. No matter how she tried, the doctors still missed their signature pages. She thought if she could invent a machine that would grab the doctor's hand and sign the pages for him, every hospital in America would buy it and she could retire at twenty-six!

"Call the transcriptionist, Jennifer. See if she still has Dr. Blaine's signature on electronic file."

"She may have it on file, but the question is, has she lost it?"

"I know, I know." Karen rolled her eyes.

Ralph knocked on the outside door. He led Taylor to the counter. Karen and Jennifer just kept working. It was only Ralph. They knew they didn't need to miss a beat.

"Karen, this is Detective Taylor."

"Ma'am."

"Don't tell me that we're that far behind on our charts that you're bringin' in the police, Dr. Peyton."

Jennifer shook her head from side to side, while Karen took another sip of orange soda. The sugar helped her stay awake late into the night. She figured from Ralph's intense look, they'd be there awhile. Ralph smirked. He took anything from Karen. The hospital couldn't run without Karen keeping track of all the paperwork of the last twenty plus years. Electronic medical records are fine, except when hundreds of patient charts get lost in cyberspace. Karen was able to retrieve each and every one on her paper backup. Thank God, Karen was old school.

"No, but don't tempt me. Does a Janelle Roamer still work here?"

"Yes, Dr. Peyton, but she took some personal time."

Ralph formed a fist with his hand and brought it to his lips. He took a deep, slow breath. Taylor pulled a pen from his shirt pocket and flipped through the mounds of scribbles in his notepad until he found an open page.

"Do you know what it's about, or where she may have gone?"

"Anything will help," Ralph asked, tugging at his eyebrow.

Karen normally didn't see Ralph like this. He never let his guard down, if at all.

"These young kids, we don't talk much; maybe Jennifer knows. Jennifer," she called out.

"Yeah, Karen." Jennifer came out from the stacks in the back where they kept the archived files. The smell of decades old charts grew stronger as Jennifer came closer to the front counter.

"Did Janelle say anything to you about this personal time she took?" Karen asked.

"She's been talking for some time about getting away, something to do with her father."

"Has she been talking about a vacation?" Ralph's words pierced the air with their intensity.

"No, just getting away, then boom, three days ago she said she had to leave right away to take care of some family business."

"Did she mention where she might be going?" Taylor pulled on the already tense muscle at the back of his neck.

Jennifer bit the side of her lip and tried to remember.

"That's the odd thing. What family business could she possibly have in Alaska?"

The kitchen staff delivered dinners for Jennifer and Karen. It was steak night, with wine sauce, garlic mashed potatoes, and baby carrots in butter. Nothing smelled good to Taylor or Ralph at this point.

THE SHERIFF'S OFFICE

Bud Richards walked up the steps of his sheriff's office. Hard to believe it was thirty years ago next month he and April packed up their three kids and left Montana for a wilder west. It had been an adventure, that's for sure. He'd been after the city groundskeeper to make him a new Larsen County sign for the front of the station. The fading green paint on the wooden edges contrasted with the steep, sharp lines of the brand new building. The townspeople just couldn't seem to let go of everything at once. It kept things nice and stable. The sign stayed and so did Bud.

It was a two-cop shop. Even though Bud and his deputy sheriff, Joe Barber, had only been in their new digs for four months, they were happy to report that the bulletin boards were strewn with random papers an inch thick. The coffee-maker spewed rotten, burnt-smelling coffee twenty-four hours a day, and the vinyl cushioned chairs had already scuffed the wooden floors beyond repair. The boys could relax. They felt at home.

Joe was glad they'd finally computerized their system. Who used typewriters after the millennium? The phone blared with a screeching ring. Thank God, this one was lower pitched than the last one.

"Deputy Sheriff Joe Barber, Larsen County. May I help you?"

It was the three p.m., midafternoon sulk. Bud strolled in and headed for the coffeemaker despite knowing he had to load up on sugar and cream to make his fine beverage palatable. Joe started taking detailed notes.

"Okay, okay...yes...Sheriff Richards just walked in. You need to talk to him right away. Let me put you on hold while I get him."

"Everything okay?" Bud set down his coffee.

"Bud, it's Doc Nolan's supervisor and some detective. They think they found the stalker."

"I'll pick it up at my desk." Bud took a seat and settled into the very loud squeak of his chair. He didn't appreciate another reminder that he needed to lose fifty pounds.

"This is Sheriff Bud Richards."

SKYE'S CABIN

The truck shook and took major bumps along the rocky back road as Sam and Janelle headed toward Skye's cabin. Janelle wore her straight blonde locks down around her shoulders. Most of the medical assistants Sam had worked with over the years wore their hair up and out of the way, even during their off hours. Sam noticed the tobacco stains on Janelle's fingertips.

"Sorry to put a dent in your plans, Dr. Nolan, but Millie made it a point that I stay with you. She wanted to make sure you were safe."

"Millie's careful that way. I'm just surprised I never met you before. It's such a small town."

Janelle kept looking straight ahead out the front window. She didn't even turn toward Sam when she spoke.

"People can be around you for a long time, and a person may not even know it."

Then Janelle turned toward Sam and smiled.

THE SHERIFF'S OFFICE

Bud waved Ray inside from the doorway. He cradled the phone between his chin and right shoulder while he grabbed a pen and paper. Ray took a seat on the edge of Joe's desk.

"Janelle Roamer, no, I haven't run across her around here." Bud furrowed his forehead.

Ray started playing with a rubber band. Bud had that "long telephone call" look on his face.

"I heard there's a brushfire going up Colby Lane, Joe." Ray picked up the wedding photo of Joe and Kate. Must have been the early years. Later on, it would be Joe and the hundred pound mackerel he caught at Deep Lake.

"Isn't that the back side of Skye's house?" Joe put his feet up on the edge of the desk.

"That's why I came—have you seen him?" Ray stuck a toothpick in his mouth.

Bud leaned forward in his chair, shaking his right knee under the table. He had gotten all the information he needed and didn't want to stay on the phone all afternoon.

"Can you send her photo by fax? Good…she might pose as a nurse or medical assistant, got it." Bud's knee finally settled down.

Bud used the county stationery, even to take notes. He'd got his butt chewed out before for not keeping accurate records.

"I'll stay on the line while you send the fax." Bud covered the receiver, and asked "Ray, has Millie hired anyone else to work at the clinic?"

Ray threw his toothpick in the trash. The mint flavor never lasted too long.

"She hasn't mentioned anyone, why?"

"It came through. Thanks." Bud pulled Janelle's photo off the fax machine. He slammed down the phone, tightened his gun belt and grabbed his sheriff's hat from the coat rack next to the side table strewn with fish and wildlife magazines.

"Let's get down there, Ray." Bud looked around for Joe while Ray raced through the front door and took a seat in Bud's newly banged up car from last night's DUI bust.

"Hey, Joe," Bud barreled out his voice.

"Yeah." Joe came out from the storeroom with a ream of copy paper.

"We don't have much time; go up Cedar Mountain Road and start evacuating the families."

Joe locked up and headed outside. Bud and Ray were already lost in the distance.

THE CLINIC

Bud and Ray rushed into the front of the clinic, the screen door slamming behind them. Millie let the incoming caller go to voicemail.

"Millie, where's Sam?" Ray had his intense look on his face.

"She and Skye delivered Miranda's baby this morning. She's on her way back."

Millie studied the squint in Ray's eye. She rose from her chair, then Bud handed her the fax with Janelle's photo.

"Has this woman been looking for Sam?" Millie stared at the photo and slumped backward into her chair. She placed her hand on her chest in disbelief.

"Why she just came in this morning sayin' Doc Sam's supervisor sent her here to work as Doc's medical assistant."

Ray leaned against the counter. "Her name is—"

"Janelle Roamer." Millie finished his sentence at the same time she turned milk white.

"We think she's the stalker."

Bud grabbed his cell phone out of his front pocket. The sound of him pressing the keys to call Joe fell into one signal of panic. Millie rubbed her forehead then slammed her fist on the desk.

"My God," she said, shaking her head with guilt.

"Where's Sam now?" Ray softened.

SKYE'S CABIN

The sound of Skye's engine beat against the silence of the grounds surrounding the cabin. Sam turned off the engine. Janelle noticed Sam place the cell phone in the cup holder. She looked away so Sam couldn't tell she was watching her every move. Janelle relished her lucky break.

Sam slammed the door of the truck behind her and jogged toward the front door. Janelle took her time getting out of the truck. The sounds of chirping birds and chainsaws on the other side of mountain surrounded them. Sam looked up to see smoke not too far in the distance.

174

"I hope we're okay here. Looks like the fire is not too far away." Sam scrambled for the key to the cabin in the bottom of her purse.

Janelle stood a few steps behind Sam. "Millie knows about it. That's why she wanted me to stay with you. She said she was going to call Skye to get here right away."

"Millie's always looking out for me." Sam scrounged the very bottom and found the key.

Janelle stepped up right next to Sam. "Let's go in. We'll be safer inside."

Janelle waited to follow Sam inside. Sam felt her parched, dry lips and headed straight for the kitchen and the cold iced tea in the fridge. Janelle stayed back. She locked the door behind them.

THE CLINIC

The afternoon sun streamed in past the clinic blinds and heated up the waiting room. Bud wiped the sweat off his brow. Millie switched the phone to voicemail.

"Dr. Sam said she was stopping at the café to pick up lunch for her and Skye."

"And then…" Bud waited for more information. Ray kept pacing the room.

"I think she said she was going to meet him at his cabin."

Millie locked up the cash receipts in the money drawer then turned out the lights to the clinic. She set the alarm system. Even their serene town had a fair share of break-ins.

"Let's go, Bud; we don't have much time." Ray waved Bud to the front door.

THE ROOSTER CAFÉ

Bud and Ray stood at the cash register waiting for Jamie. Only midafternoon customers searching for their second wind with a pick-me-up of caffeine and sugar via blueberry pie filled the red plastic booths.

"Jamie," Ray called.

"Hi Ray, Bud. Everything okay, guys?" Jamie threw her bar towel over her shoulder.

"Jamie, has Dr. Sam been here yet today?" Bud noticed the kids twirling around on the counter stools. He checked to make sure the safety was on his gun.

"She just left less than fifteen minutes ago." She washed her hands then wiped them dry. She felt the deep cracks between her fingers from years of industrial soap and hard water.

Bud handed Jamie Janelle's photo. "Has this woman been here today looking for Dr. Sam?"

Jamie reached for her eyeglasses from under the counter and put them on.

"I think she's the one who came in and just walked up to Dr. Sam and started talking to her. I called Millie, and she said she was up here to work with Dr. Sam. Something about Dr. Sam's boss sending her to help out."

"What happened?" Ray leaned forward.

"You're scaring me. Is Dr. Sam all right?"

"Did they stay or leave?" Bud turned down the volume of the radio on his shoulder.

"Next thing I saw was this woman in the parking lot getting into Skye's truck with Dr. Sam."

Bud pulled his car keys out of his pocket. "Did you see which way they were headed?" he asked.

"They were going up Canyon Road." Jamie began to tremble.

Ray cocked his head to one side and signaled Bud. "Let's go. They're at Skye's cabin."

SKYE'S CABIN

Janelle made herself comfortable in the leather sofa in front of Skye's fireplace. She imagined how many times Skye and Sam would have talked into the early morning hours, laughing and trying not to glance at each other. She watched Sam work her way around the kitchen. Must be nice to have a special person so close as long as your luck didn't run out.

"Would you like a soda, iced tea, or some juice?" Sam hollered from behind the refrigerator door.

"Anything is good." Janelle hesitated. "On second thought, do you have any lemonade?"

"I'll have to check the other fridge."

Sam headed out the back door of the kitchen toward the garage. Janelle waited until she heard the garage door open. She pulled her wire cutters out of her jacket pocket and cut the phone lines. She made it back to the sofa just before she heard the rustle of feet.

"I swear Skye's a typical male. There's mostly beer in these refrigerators."

"Water's okay." Janelle flipped through the Outdoor Life magazine in the copper bin next to the end table. Sam walked in with the beverages.

"Here you go."

"Thanks."

Janelle felt the ice-cold condensation against her warm hand. She ran the glass across her forehead to cool herself down. Sam settled into the corduroy chair and a half where Skye normally read. Janelle watched the sides come up and hug Sam.

"I'm still surprised I've never run into you before. I've been up here almost six weeks now." Sam shook her glass and the melting ice sank to the bottom.

"I was away for a while, taking care of some family business. Just got back into town."

Janelle took a long sip of her water and peered over her glass at Sam. "My father died."

"Oh, I'm sorry. I didn't know. Was it sudden?" Sam kicked off her shoes and tucked her legs under herself to get more comfortable. She tensed up and rubbed her shoulders to get warmer. The room felt cold. Janelle avoided looking at the telephone and gazed around the walls. Skye's hunting trophies seemed ironic, since he was on the other side of the coin now. She brought herself around, back to Sam.

"Yes, a heart attack. Died almost instantly when he got to the emergency room." Janelle sucked on an ice cube, then spit it back into her glass. "The doctor on call couldn't revive him."

Sam put her drink down on the end table between them. She dropped her smile and relaxed her face. She'd done that so many times it came automatic to her now.

"I'm sorry for your loss. Before I came up here, I worked in the emergency room at our regional hospital. I saw a lot of that. It's never easy, no matter what the circumstances are."

Janelle pushed Sam's iced tea out of the way and set her glass on the end table.

"I'm sure you did. You can understand then." Janelle raised the corners of her mouth into a forced smile.

Sam's cell phone sat in the car. All the messages went to voicemail.

THE FIRE

The SUV shook forward and backward over the potholes and rough patches in the road as Bud and Ray raced toward the fire.

"Turn left up here, Bud; we can take Sand Road to get to

Skye's." Bud picked up the radio and turned up the volume as high as he could.

"All units within twenty miles of Woodbridge, we have an armed and dangerous stalker at Skye Ronan's cabin."

Ray pointed to outside the driver's side window. "Look ahead, Bud. That wildfire will be at Skye's front door in less than ten minutes."

The red paint of the fire trucks stood out against the black and gray smoke of the line of fire inching itself along the roadside. The high-pitched screams of the sirens didn't even phase the crows flying in every different direction. This was a logging community. They were used to mayhem.

Billie and Rich waved from the lead fire truck to Jim and Dan in the backup behind them. Everyone was loaded up with gear and wiping the sweat off their brows, only to be replaced by the residue in the air. Billie parked the fire truck and got out to survey the edge of the canyon. The normally serene contours of the evergreens were replaced by a charging orange and blue stream in full force. There was no tranquility today.

"It's heading toward the mountainside," Billie shouted to Rich.

"Dammit, I think we better call the smoke jumpers."

Rich grabbed the fire truck radio and signaled Jim and Dan to start up their rig again.

Ray had never seen it get this bad before. They'd had wildfires in Woodbridge in much drier seasons, but nothing this insurmountable. Bud grabbed the binoculars out of the back of his SUV and focused the lenses on the road directly across the canyon from them. He spotted the fire trucks and watched them race to get to the head of the blaze. Time seemed as elusive as a rushing river. Bud pulled his walkie-talkie off his belt.

"Joe—come in, Joe."

"Yeah, Bud," Joe responded, through a scratchy background. "I'm up here evacuating the families."

"Get the families to help you get everyone out. We're losing time. Head toward Skye's cabin now. This stalker has too much time."

"I'm leaving right now, Bud."

Ray shielded his eyes from the blazing sun. The breeze against his face felt cool and soothing but it would fuel the fire some more.

"Can we get more help?" Ray asked Bud.

Bud pressed the walkie-talkie button harder in frustration.

"Once again, calling all backup units within twenty miles of Woodbridge." Bud's voice popped up on a motorcycle cop's radio.

"We have an armed and dangerous stalker at Skye Ronan's cabin, 24316 Canyon Road. Please respond."

The motorcycle cop checked his mirrors to see if there was anyone behind him. He spun 180 degrees, almost hitting the ground, and tore off toward the canyon.

SKYE'S CABIN

Janelle sat at the end of the sofa, closer to Sam's chair. She was getting warm. She unzipped her jacket, but wouldn't take it off. Sam stared at the clock on the mantle over the fireplace. She could hear the gears move each second forward. Janelle picked up the photo of Ray and Skye off the yellowed lace cloth embedded into the antique oak end table.

"Do you know this Skye well?" Janelle gave the picture frame to Sam.

"Not really." Sam placed the photo back on the table. "But I'd like to know him better."

Janelle stretched out her arms and emitted a loud yawn, like she was just waking up.

"It's great to have a man in your life to love."

Janelle stood up and strolled in front of the fireplace. When she got to the end, she picked up the poker from the fireplace tools.

"Mine was my Dad. My whole world crashed the day he died." The fireplace poker fell out of Janelle's hands. The hard brass metal crashed onto the tile in front of the fireplace.

Sam flinched, and straightened up her shoulders. "A terrible loss for you."

Janelle picked up the poker, but instead of putting back it back with the other fireplace tools, she sat down in the chair furthest from Sam. She started tapping the end of the poker in her open hand, a steady rhythm, never missing a beat.

"The doctors, they say they tried, that they 'did all they could,' then they just gave up and went on to the next person."

Sam turned on the lamp. She wanted to get a better look at the expression on Janelle's face. She took her time twisting the knob at the end of the light bulb, so she could estimate the best route to the front door.

"They must have done CPR for a while, medications, shocked him with the defibrillator?"

Sam looked straight at Janelle. She wanted to keep the conversation going. Janelle's face turned ice cold.

"She, she did all those things, and then she said, 'I'm sorry for your loss' just like you did now."

Janelle stopped tapping the poker in her open hand. She tightened her grip on the handle until her knuckles turned white and Sam could see every tendon bulging out from her fist.

"These situations are so tragic, it's hard for physicians to know what to say or do to console families," Sam replied in a lowered tone.

Sam planted both feet firmly in front of her and leaned forward in her chair.

"It's not hard for doctors to leave someone you love dead on a table, then walk away like it has no meaning." Janelle paused. "Did it, Dr. Nolan?"

Sam sprinted toward the front door but felt the cold metal against her legs knock her down. She tried to get up, but the back of Janelle's hand slapped her down. Sam opened her eyes and through the blood streaming down the side of her face she lay looking at the barrel of Pete's gun.

"Of course you don't recognize it. Pete bought it for you, but he never got it to you did he? So now I have it." Janelle laughed.

Sam tried to edge backward, but every time she moved an inch, Janelle stuck Pete's gun in her ribs.

"Don't worry, you're not the one I'm going to kill with it."

Janelle picked up the photo of Ray and Skye, then threw it into the fireplace. The glass fragments scattered everywhere leaving razor sharp edges like daggers.

"I wonder where he is right now."

૨૯

Skye felt every one of his breaths pushing against the inside of his chest wall as he ran toward the fire heading to his cabin. He took off his shirt and threw it down, only to reveal his T-shirt drenched with perspiration across his chest and neck. His face grew more flushed as he neared the massive wall of flames.

૨૯

Sam rubbed her forehead and could feel the growing lump from the impact.

"My God," she mumbled through her daze.

Janelle pulled up a side chair and leaned forward as she talked down to Sam.

"We can be around people every day and not even know they're there."

Sam rubbed her eyes and Janelle came into focus. Sam locked her gaze on Janelle without letting go. Janelle's face seemed plain and dull from this angle. Janelle pulled a pack of cigarettes out of her inside pocket and lit one. She blew the smoke right in Sam's face.

"They can clean up your mess in an emergency room after a gun-wielding psycho shoots it up for drugs, huh, Doc?"

Janelle brushed her hair back from her shoulders and leaned back in her chair, twisting the ends in tight ringlets with her free hand. She remembered back to that day when she bent down on the ER floor to pick up the pieces of broken glass from the smashed supply jars.

Sam remembered coming in to retrieve her cell phone. The day's crazed substance abuser was yet again the last straw for Sam who noticed the slim, blonde woman in front of her from the back and shook her head. Miserable job, she had thought, having to clean up after doctors, nurses, and nasty patients. She had headed down the corridor, unbeknownst to her with Janelle close behind.

Sam tried to get up, but Janelle kicked her back down.

"They can push over a shelf in the library and scare us half to death." Janelle had lowered her voice to a long whisper. "They can even murder our best friend, and get away with it."

Sam took a deep breath and let out a roar as she dragged herself up and grabbed the telephone. "I'm calling Millie."

"Go ahead and dial, phone's dead."

Janelle headed toward the front door and leaned against it. Sam checked all her pockets. Janelle let out another yawn. "Poor girl, you left your cell phone in Skye's truck."

Janelle pointed the gun at Sam's forehead and they both stood still. The silence was broken when Janelle cocked back the trigger.

"Not so tough now, Doc, are we?" I won't shoot you in the head. The last time I did that Tommy's brains went all over the room. That was way too much of a mess for even someone like me to clean up."

"You're sick, if you hadn't noticed."

Janelle slapped Sam in the face with her gun. "Watch your language, Doc. You're a professional—be polite."

"What's wrong with you? Your father died of a heart attack. There's nothing more I could've done for him. Nothing anyone could have done," she shouted.

"He had a name, Larry Dwyer, and he's all I had." Sam felt Janelle's boot in the curve of her spine.

"I did everything I possibly could do to save him," she moaned. Sam lifted her chin and felt the barrel of the gun against her throat when she swallowed.

"Think back, Doc. Think back, you'll remember."

Sam had never met Lorraine Nestor, the woman who stood outside the ER trauma room. Her tears were running down her ruddy complexion, pouring onto her one cashmere sweater. It was her favorite, a gift from Larry the previous Christmas. He always bragged how he had saved up until he could afford to dress her like a real lady.

Sam watched Lorraine cup her face in her hands. The tears had washed away her makeup to show the wrinkles of many years of sacrifice she had shared with Larry.

"I'm sorry for your loss." Sam threw her stethoscope around her neck and motioned to the ER nurse she would be coming into the next room.

"Can you speak with his daughter? She's on her way."

Lorraine rubbed the fine weave of the cashmere sweater. She wanted to keep it perfect. It was a small, but precious, memory of Larry.

Janelle came rushing down the ER hallway. As she grew closer and Lorraine's tears became more visible to her, the heels of her shoes struck heavier and faster on the ER floor.

"I'm sorry, ma'am, I have to go. I have another patient emergency to tend to."

Sam left, leaving Lorraine alone outside Larry's room. Lorraine lifted her eyes to face Janelle. She shook her head from side to side and Janelle screamed.

Janelle stood over Sam and threw one of Skye's wooden carved lamps across the living room of the cabin.

"You couldn't even spend thirty seconds to talk to me," Janelle screamed in an anguished voice. "I lose the man who's most important to me in this world and you can't give me thirty seconds of your time." Janelle raised her hand to strike Sam again.

"No, get away from me!" Sam shrieked.

Skye heard the screaming from inside the cabin. He tore through the shrubs to get to the front door. The lock wouldn't open. He turned the metal knob side by side, but it wouldn't budge. Janelle turned her head for a split second to see Skye's figure through the lace curtain draped on the back of the door. Sam struck Janelle on the side of head and wrestled her to the ground. Skye broke a glass pane in the door and opened it from the inside.

Janelle and Sam were both crawling on the floor toward the gun, which had fallen out of Janelle's hand. Sam reached for it and was able to grab it with Janelle on top of her. Skye lunged forward, but Janelle grabbed Sam's wrist and inched her way up to squeeze Sam's resistant fingers on the trigger. A loud pop filled the air and Sam saw Skye fall to the ground, reaching for his leg.

"Oh God, Skye." Sam's heart fell to her feet.

Janelle sat up and cocked the barrel at Skye's head while Sam applied pressure to the wound. She ripped open the bloody jeans at the bullet site and tied her belt around Skye's muscular calf.

"Hello. You must be Skye." Janelle lowered the gun and took a seat.

THE FIRE

The lights of the fire trucks blended in with the orange flames of the advancing fire. Billie, Rich, and Jimmy with their full, weighted-down gear were the new kids on the block. Even though Dan had thirty years on each of them, he trusted them with his life. Today he had no choice. They were the only ones up there. Dan focused his binoculars and watched the fire rage past the clear-cut meadow. It would slow down the flames, but not for long. Skye's cabin was now in full view.

"Jimmy, Billie, get those hoses hooked up," Dan shouted.

"Got it." Billie cracked open the water source.

"I'm going up the ladder." Jimmy's boots made a loud bang against the metal steps. Rich pulled ahead, wearing his protective gear.

"We can't get to Skye's house from here, Dan." He waved from the brush.

"Rich, I'm radioing the smoke jumpers now." Dan raised his arm and circled it to cue Rich to turn on the hose. How much time could he buy for Skye?

SKYE'S CABIN

Janelle stood by the bay window and watched the fire steer toward the cabin. She noticed the fire trucks in the distance, but they weren't moving any closer. She could relax, but only a little. Trusting no one always made her stay alert. She didn't care; she hadn't planned for this meeting to last a long time.

"I really didn't want a lot of people to attend this party." Janelle grabbed Sam by the arm and dragged her up. Sam was still holding on to Skye.

"Christ, you shot him in the leg. I need to stop the bleeding and get him out of here."

"Get up, both of you, now, and head toward the back door. We're goin' for a hike."

THE FIRE

Bud and Ray raced into the stream of fire trucks. No sooner did they get out of their SUV than they started to choke from the wave of smoke moving toward Skye's cabin. The lower doors from the smoke jumper planes blasted open to release a load of extinguisher that followed the wind until everyone on the mountaintop could taste the bitterness in the air. Even the team trying to clear the brush felt the hot poker of the branches gnaw into their skin as they rushed closer into the valley. Ray covered his nose and mouth with a cloth, to lessen the stench of the charred woods around him.

"Dan, we need to get to Skye's cabin," Bud yelled over the screaming sirens.

"No way, Bud, I can't let you past here. Looks like Skye's going to lose his cabin."

Dan waved the front team back in before the fire could get to them first. Ray put his makeshift mask in his pocket. He stood silent and watched the mass of embers overtake everything in their path, shaking his head in frustration.

"Skye's going to lose a lot more than that," Ray sighed.

THE MOUNTAINTOP

Sam pulled Skye up the mountainside with barely enough strength for herself. Janelle kept her gun in close range of Sam's face. The metal barrel seemed to be heating up, even though the flames hadn't reached them yet. When she couldn't pull any longer, Sam pushed Skye as hard as she could. His strong arms and upper body tryed to help her move them along, but even he was running out of steam. Janelle checked behind her to see the fire trying to catch up to them.

"Go faster you two, or I'll shoot the other leg. Then you can carry him, Doc."

Janelle felt the sweat pour out from under her jacket and clothes. She shielded her eyes from the sunlight, but was still able to see the congregation of fire trucks and cop cars in the distance. Sam and Skye could smell the air turning burnt with every heavy breath they took.

"This is Alaska. I thought you people were supposed to be rugged? Pick up the pace, lovebirds."

Janelle took off her coat and threw it to the side, fanning her clothes from the heat.

SKYE'S CABIN

Bud stood on the side of the road. The wind was picking up and he could hear the tree branches sway in unison. He left Ray with Dan, but knew he had to get closer in to Skye's cabin. He tried to get there the back way, but the site was still blocked by a recent mudslide.

"Joe, Joe, come in Joe." Bud shook the walkie-talkie.

"Yeah, Bud," came the voice barely audible from the other end.

"Where are you?" Bud turned to get better reception.

"I'm on Cedar Mountain Road. I can see Skye's cabin."

Bud could hear Joe's tires ride roughshod over the terrain, right through the walkie-talkie. He was glad now that he fought with the mayor to get him that truck for the department, even if it was a gas-guzzler.

"Get up there now, Joe. We think the stalker's got Skye and Dr. Sam at the cabin."

Joe didn't wait for anyone. He kicked in the front door and checked all the rooms. As soon as he saw the fireplace poker and the lamp knocked over, he headed straight to the back door. Sam and Skye were struggling to get up the back of the mountainside with Janelle close behind. Joe shook his walkie-talkie, but couldn't cut the static.

"I see them. I'm heading up the mountainside from the back of Skye's cabin."

Joe turned down the volume of his walkie-talkie, cocked his gun and crouched down as he followed them in his ascent.

"Joe, Joe. Dammit!" Bud moved out of the crowd of noisy fire trucks and shouting firemen to a relatively open space.

"What is it, Bud?" Ray guzzled a half bottle of ice water and poured the rest over his head.

"These archaic radios. I lost reception. I think Joe found 'em." Ray pointed to the peak across the valley, barely visible at its base from the raging inferno.

"If you lost reception, that means he's heading up the mountainside, back of Skye's cabin. We can drive to Cedar Mountain Road, and hike up the rest."

"I can't take you up there Ray. You don't have a gun."

Ray pulled back his jacket and flashed Bud his holster with his favorite pistol.

"Let's go, Bud. This is Alaska, everybody has a gun."

Ray and Bud followed the old railroad highway toward the woods behind Skye's cabin. They had always been tucked away and safe from fires, at least until today.

THE CHASE

Joe slid behind a group of rocks, which allowed him to keep an eye on Janelle. From where he stood, he knew Skye was hurt, but couldn't tell how bad. He tried to step out to keep following them, but stepped on some broken twigs. Janelle turned, but Joe's reflexes were quicker. He ducked down without taking a breath.

"Keep moving, you two. All the way up." Janelle gave Skye a push from behind.

Janelle, Skye, and Sam were just minutes from the top, when Joe checked every space between him and them. He knew he was running out of time. He eased his way out into the open, but caught a stone, which started a rumbling beneath him. Janelle looked over. Joe fired and missed, but Janelle was able to get one into Joe's shoulder. He fell back and rushed to cover underneath a shrub.

Bud and Ray stood outside Skye's cabin and followed the gunshots. Ray ran past the side of the house.

"It came from behind the cabin."

"They're heading up the mountain. Stay behind me, Ray." Bud pulled his gun.

They followed the worn path and stayed in Joe's tracks. He saw them from afar and they motioned him to stay down.

Sam huddled Skye as close to her chest as she could. She kept pressure on his leg. Sweat poured across his brow and drenched his shirt. The mountaintop rose over the fumes and flames like a bell tower. The woods opened up to a clearing that had a crystal clear view of the town. The wind had finally died down. Sam and Skye lay still. All was silent, but not serene.

Janelle sat off to the side and rested on a thick, decomposing log.

"This is such a lovely place for all of us to die. Look at that view. Doesn't it just make you feel closer to God?"

Janelle grabbed Skye by the front of his shirt and dragged him close to her. She let go and he started falling down the embankment until Sam caught him.

"Stop it, you crazed lunatic. He's injured."

"Wow, you figured that out? No wonder they made you a doctor." Janelle laughed.

Janelle stood over them. Her blank stare turned white. She put the gun to Skye's head.

"What does it feel like, Doc, to stand there and watch while someone you love is going to die?"

Sam put herself between Skye and Janelle. "Stop it, please! He's not a part of this. It's between you and me."

Ray and Bud found the shrub-laden path up to the clearing. The broad cedars made a dark tunnel to hide them from Janelle. Ray eyed Joe, who was now rolled up into a ball between two bushes holding his shoulder.

"Joe, it's Ray. I'm here with Bud. Where'd she get you?" Joe released the pressure on his shoulder.

"It's a flesh wound. I think I can make it down without her seeing me."

"Get down to base and see if you can radio state patrol to send a sharpshooter to the other side of the canyon. He may be able to pick off the stalker if she steps away from Skye and Dr. Sam," Bud ordered.

"Got it." Joe waited until a breeze came through to make some distracting noise, then took off down the trail.

Bud peered around the edge of the dirt path and took a few steps. He saw the three of them ahead. He signaled to Ray. They each broke open into the sunlight and followed opposite directions.

THE CLEARING

Janelle brushed her gun gently over Sam's chin.

"Oh, but you're wrong, Doc. He's very much a part of this. See, I want you to feel. To feel what it's like to have someone you love so dearly be taken away from you."

Janelle stroked Skye's temple with the gun. He tightened his lips and shut his eyes to avoid eye contact with Janelle. Time, he needed to buy them more time. Janelle lifted her gun to make a circular motion. The circle got larger with each second.

"That's the only way we can complete the circle."

Sam shifted her footing and felt a lump in her coat brush up against her right hip. She followed the edge of the jacket backward with her right hand, but stayed fixed on Janelle.

She kept talking. "I don't understand. How does killing him do any good?"

"Can't you see?" Janelle smiled. "Then you and I will always be connected, Doc, bound forever. I lose the man I loved most in this world, and you do too."

Sam pushed her right hand against her pocket. Like a child's game of guessing the object under the velvet cloth, she made it out as Miranda's brooch. She had completely forgotten about it until now.

Janelle grabbed Sam by the neck. Sam's arms wrestled from side to side until she stopped fighting. At least that's what Janelle thought.

"I kept you guessing who was chasing you all this time, didn't I? Amazing what fate will reveal to you over time."

"Yes, how true." Sam smiled.

Janelle didn't notice that Sam couldn't take her eyes off Skye as she spoke. Sam cradled Skye as close to her as she could while keeping pressure on the wound. She felt an eerie calm holding Skye.

THE CLIFF

The cop slowed down his motorcycle as he approached the front of the mountainside. He could see all of them off in the distance. He killed his engine when he reached the base. He took off his helmet and figured his uniform was enough to show he was a cop. He didn't need to add more signals. He bent forward and edged toward a group of trees just shading the mountaintop.

Sam's hands stopped trembling. She brushed her hair to one side and let the incoming breeze stroke her now sore neck. The wind had shifted and it felt cooler. The smell of charred wood seemed to be floating away, bringing back the pine scent. The crackling of the fire faded away, like the quiet of the last wave following an ocean storm.

Sam lowered her voice and slowed her speech. "I guess you're right, you win."

"What?" Janelle stiffened her shoulders. "No way. I know you. You don't give up that easy."

Sam took a few steps away from Skye, knowing Janelle would follow.

"It's not him you want to kill, it's me. It's me you hate, so why drag him into this fight? Go ahead," Sam challenged, lifting her arms up at both sides, signaling Janelle to come closer.

"What are you talking about?" Janelle tightened the grip on her gun. She could taste salt on her lips they were so parched.

Sam kept inching herself farther out of the clearing and toward the cliff. She cocked her head to signal Skye to stay down. She wouldn't stop walking away from Janelle, urging her to follow her steps at the same time. Sam knew Janelle hadn't come this far not to take the bait. She stopped within a few feet of the slope leading to the jagged rocks below.

"You want to complete the circle, let him go and kill me. Then you'll get what you really want." Sam shoved her hands in her pockets. "Just like you said, Janelle—bound, forever."

The motorcycle cop turned off his radio. The last thing he needed was the abrupt sound of his station chief blasting over the airwaves. He finally got Janelle in range, but she kept moving from side to side, like a nervous butterfly. She was right in between Sam and Skye. He drew his gun anyway.

"Nice try, but he's going first, Doc." Janelle's voice missed a beat for the first time.

Bud and Ray reunited at the top behind a group of large tree stumps, the remnants of the last forest fire before this one. Ray pulled his inhaler from his pocket and took a few deep puffs to fight off the altitude change. He peered upward over the flat top of their barrier. Lucky for them his dark hair blended into the wooded background.

"I can't get a shot," Ray whispered.

"Dammit, neither can I." Bud rounded the corner of the edges of the bark, but he couldn't get his gun in the right position.

Janelle stepped back so she was facing both Sam and Skye. She lifted her gun to a direct shot at Skye's forehead, which was now shaking up and down from his heavy breathing. She used her free hand to steady the trembling of her aim.

"I just wanna see your face when you lose the man you love." Janelle raised her eyes in question. "You do love him, don't you, Doc?"

Sam kept her right hand in her pocket and tightened her left fist behind her back. At no time in her life did she want to show emotion more than at this moment. She knew if Janelle had any idea of her true feelings toward Skye, it would endanger him more.

"Answer me!" Janelle demanded.

Skye's face blended into the peaceful scenery behind him, also waiting for an answer.

A shot rang out from the motorcycle cop's pistol, but missed Janelle and echoed from the canyon below. Janelle turned her gun toward Sam thinking this would be her only split second to act. It came down to this one chance for Sam. She threw Miranda's brooch straight into Janelle's temple, then rushed forward. Janelle fell to her knees at the same time she dropped her gun over the mountaintop and out of sight. Janelle clawed her way up and gave Sam a right hook to the chest.

Bud and Ray split up onto opposite sides of Sam and Janelle. All four were caught up in a slow moving dance, but neither Bud nor Ray could get a shot off. They were too close. Janelle and Sam wrestled to the edge of the cliff, just inches from falling into the crevice. Skye rolled backward, unconscious. Sam coughed and wheezed in between Janelle's choking motions on her neck. Bud finally couldn't wait any longer. He cocked back his gun only to hear Sam give one last kick to Janelle's chest, which lifted her up and into the air, over the side of the mountaintop.

Sam sat up to breathe, only to drop her head in her hands after seeing Janelle's crumpled body lying on the rocks far below.

"Doc, you okay?" Bud rushed to Sam to help her up.

"Skye, Skye. My God, are you all right?" She rushed to Skye and could see him still breathing. She knelt down and checked his carotid pulse. It was even and strong. She took his hand in hers and turned away from Bud and Ray. She didn't want them to see her crying. Skye opened his eyes. He'd never seen such softness in Sam's face. A welcome sight, following this nightmare. He reached up and wiped away the tears from her face.

"You're here. That makes everything all right." He smiled.

Sam took off her jacket and brushed the rest of the leaves and twigs off her body. She gave Bud a big hug.

"No, Bud, at the moment I'm not okay." Then she looked at Skye. "But I will be."

"I saw everything, Doc. It was gonna be you or her," Bud reassured Sam.

Ray ran to Skye and leaned over his bloodstained pants. Skye was finally able to catch his breath.

"It's okay, Ray. Just give me your shirt so I can plug the bleeding."

"Hell, Skye, you're my employee. You're supposed to give me the shirt off your back."

Skye laughed, but not before he gave Ray a slap on the side of the head.

The late afternoon light nearly blinded the motorcycle cop's sunglasses. He picked up his radio and motioned to Bud and Ray.

"I'll radio the fire department to get the medics up here. You're gonna need help getting him down," he shouted.

Sam and Bud caught Ray leaning over Skye. Sam quickened her pace, only to find the two of them laughing like a pair of teenagers after a wild night out. Skye relished Sam's irritated smile.

"Any chance you still have office hours when we get back down this mountain?" he asked.

"I may be able to work you in," Sam replied, picking up Miranda's brooch amidst the dirt and leaves.

THE CLINIC

Millie took her usual seat as the grande dame in the clinic. The whole town wouldn't work right without her, let alone the clinic. Bud and Ray wanted to smoke their favorite cigars, but Millie put her foot down and said none in the clinic. Although the ordeal had come to an end, it was bittersweet and not a time for celebration. Everyone was exhausted. The tension from the recent events was slowly diluted away by humor and ribbing.

Joe Barber couldn't do a whole lot of anything. His shoulder hurt from the gunshot wound and was wrapped in a sling. It didn't stop him from using his other arm to grab a cigar from Bud's shirt pocket. The whole crew sighed a big chorus of relief when Sam brought Skye out to the reception area in a wheelchair.

"I always said you'd get old before me, Skye." Ray laughed.

"If you guys start having wheelchair races, I want twenty percent of the winnin's from both of you," Millie warned, slamming her hand on the desk.

"It's worth turning a blind eye to that," Bud joked.

Bud saw the relief and lingering fear in Sam's eyes. She gave Bud an unexpected, but welcome bear hug. "Thanks, Bud," she said. Sam squeezed Bud's arm in reassurance. "You too, Ray and Joe."

Joe lifted his arm out of the sling and waved it toward Sam.

"You better appreciate this, Dr. Sam. It's my bowling arm."

Sam wiped her brow and let out a deep sigh. She had never in her life experienced such a grueling and frightening challenge as this. She couldn't think of anybody but those people in this room whom she would want watching her back. Is this what it felt like to belong?

"Doc, I know you feel guilty about all this, but you had no choice." Bud leaned against the counter while Skye wheeled himself over to the conversation.

"She had a choice, Bud. I'm just glad it was the one to save my life." Skye kept his focus on Sam, no matter how much she tried to look away.

"You know what you have to do now?" Ray asked.

"I don't like the sound of this," Sam replied. For the first time she was in a room full of people and had the least idea of what was going on.

Millie started turning off the lights to close up.

"When Skye gets back on his feet, you have to go back."

"Go back?"

"Yes, go back to the top of the mountain," Bud answered.

"But why?"

"All the loggers do it when the mountain gives you a big challenge." Skye took Sam's hand. "To face your fears."

THE MOUNTAINTOP

It was a much clearer day and a lot warmer than their last trip up. Sam and Skye were almost to the very top, only slowed down by Skye's limp. The clearing was empty now and quiet, no rescue team. It had rained the night before so everything looked green and smelled even greener.

"We made it." Sam reached out to Skye to make the last step to the top.

"Yes, we did." Skye took off his sunglasses. He didn't want to miss one moment of Sam in the bright light.

"I'm up here. Guess I faced my fears after all."

"Not quite." Skye shook his head.

"What do you mean, not quite?"

"Do you remember the last thing Janelle said to you?"

"She wanted to see my face before she killed you."

"She asked you a question, but you didn't answer her." Skye set down his cane and walked over to Sam. He put his arms around her and pulled her closer to him. "She said she wanted to see your face when you lost the man you love. She asked you, 'You do love him, Doc?'"

Sam kissed Skye's forehead, then his cheeks, then his eyes, ears, and neck, everywhere but his lips.

"…don't you…" Skye went on.

Sam cradled Skye's face in her hands.

"Then she said, 'answer now.' But you didn't."

Sam pressed his lips onto her own. "I'm answering now."

Skye held every inch of Sam against his body, telling himself to never let go.

"Keep talking," Skye encouraged, this from a man who was always at a loss for words, except for this day. He now loved words, her words.

Sam felt the brush of the new day's sun against her face. Skye tightened his embrace as the moments passed. It kept her warm and secure.